T0197247

My Mama
Cherry Etta

My Mama
Cherry Etta

Wanda Rhodes

MY MAMA CHERRY ETTA

iUniverse books may be ordered through booksellers or by contacting:

iUniverse
1663 Liberty Drive
Bloomington, IN 47403
www.iuniverse.com
1-800-Authors (1-800-288-4677)

ISBN: 978-1-5320-5158-6 (sc)
ISBN: 978-1-5320-5159-3 (e)

Library of Congress Control Number: 2018906507

Print information available on the last page.

iUniverse rev. date: 05/31/2018

Acknowledgements

This book is dedicated to the people who
I love
My husband Arnold (John) Rhodes
My son Arnold (Scoopy) Rhodes
My Sister Isabell Rachel (Nanny) Vester
Thank you my beautiful Niece Julia Rhodes
Special thanks to my cousin Ronnie Williams

Author's Note

This book is fiction it was inspired by my imagination.
The characters portrayed in this book are
not real the characters were made up in my
mind. If some characters seems like it's about
your life, it's not this book is fiction.

Foreword

THIS BOOK IS ABOUT a young black girl only fourteen year old having a baby boy by a White man who lives in Walnut Mississippi. She falls in love with him have a baby by him not knowing how to take care of a baby, she never went to school; she had to learn what her mother taught her and what she learn from the streets. When the baby is five years old the baby father Robert moves her and her family to Oklahoma City. He move her on N E Second street and their whole life change she loved hanging out on the street, her baby daddy Robert go to find her and he find her at a club call Deep Duce, when he walk in he see the club is full of blacks, dancing eating and having so much fun. He felt scared, all eyes is on him. Robert looks over and sees Cherry kissing on another man. Robert is so hurt he turns around and leaves. Robert take her son away from her It hurt her so bad, she leaves Oklahoma City and move to a town call Derry Oklahoma, years later she kill the man she left with and need her son to come help her. Robert never told his son he had a black mother name Cherry Etta Jackson because his son looked white. Cherry Etta mama Cora get in touch with her grandson who grew up to be a lawyer to go to Derry Oklahoma to save his mother life. Her son Henry don't understand what Cora is talking about he think she is a crazy black woman not knowing what she is talking about. When he asks his father he is shock that his father tells him it's true his Mama is black. He wants to go to meet his mother and help her. But his father want him to stay away from her he fell his son will be hurt and confused beaning around his black family.

I WAS BORN IN WALNUT Mississippi to Robert Charles Wilson and Cherry Etta Jackson. My father is a white man and my mama is a black woman. My father fell in love with her when she was fourteen years old and he was eighteen. When she was fourteen I was born. Father is a very handsome man he weight one hundred thirty seven pound he is 6'2, he have light brown hair and gray eyes. Cherry Etta weight one hundred and twenty eight pounds and have black hair, brown eyes. She was a real pretty young black girl and my father loved her. He would come and get her from the shack at night and take her to the big house where he lived. Grandma Cora and Grandpa Jackson lived and work on his plantation. They were afraid of my father and were mad at him for taking their daughter with him and knowing what he was doing to their child, whenever he wanted to come for Cherry. After a while no one cared that he would come doing the day or night to get her. January 14, 1920 I was born, they name me Henry Lee Wilson. Five years later my father decided he wanted to leave Mississippi and move to Oklahoma City. He told Cherry Etta he was leaving and taking me with him. She begs him not to take me from her; she wanted me to stay with her, because she didn't think she would ever see me again. Robert told her she could come with him and she could help take care of me while he works. Cherry Etta, mama beg Robert not to take her only child she loved her too much to be taken from her. Robert told my grandma to come with him and she could help out with Cherry Etta and me. When they were getting in the car, my grandpa Jackson got in the car with us he didn't want to be left behind. When we got to Oklahoma City father found a house on N E Second Street and we moved in it. Blacks didn't want a white man living in their neighborhood they were making fun of him with Mama so father moved across Robertson Street so he could be near us. He found a job at a book store. He would come and give my Grandma money, and help all he could. When I go outside to play with the kids, they would call me white boy and laugh at me because I had gray eyes.

One boy threw a rock at me and told me to go home with my White daddy. The kids kept bulling me so I would stay in the house until my mama would go outside. When it was time for me to go to School my mama took me to a school name Dumber Elementary. They told her that a white boy couldn't go to their school. Cherry told them that I was black and I was her son they laugh at her and told her she must be crazy. One lady (said) girl you need to take that boy over there to one of them white schools. They won't know the different. You need to have your ass in school what you doing with that white boy any way, where is his mama? My mama (said) bitch you kiss my ass and we left. I did look white I had light brown hair and gray eyes like my father. I cried a lot because the black kids would laugh at me. My father met a white girl that worked at the book store. He fell in love with her and they were married. I cried a lot because I miss my father and living in a neighborhood where I wasn't welcome. One day he came to see me he told Cherry Etta he came to get me to live with him. He knew I was not happy living in the neighborhood. She hugs me and said she would always love me. And she would come see me all the time. Father told her he was married and it would be best if she didn't come to see me because it would only confuse me. Cherry Etta started to cry and told him he couldn't do that to her. And he couldn't keep her away from me because she was my Mama. Cherry let me tell you one damn thing this is my son. And you heard what I said. Father told me to come on with him. I was glad because I didn't want to live with them on Second Street any more I wanted to go with him. Before I got in the car I heard my father said to her, he didn't' want any of them to come for me or see me and he mean every word he said. Grandma and Grandpa Jackson hug me good bye. Grandma said

God bless you child. I remember Cherry Etta saying to father. Charles I love

I want to see my son. Father didn't say a word. I was happy to leave them; the kids would never call me white boy or bully me again. Father drove up in front of this nice white house with a drive way with beautiful flowers in the yard. He said son this is your new home. I couldn't believe I was going to live in this nice house it was nothing like the house on Second Street. When I got out of the car some kids were playing ball they call and said hello what's your name can you come and play with us. Father told then maybe later. When I got in the house I saw this pretty white lady standing there with a beautiful smile on her face. You must be Henry Lee (she said) She asks me if I was hungry or need something to drink. No thank you (I said). Come and let me show you around the house and to your room. When I got to my room she said this is your room. I couldn't believe it was so nice the bed looked so nice there were curtains that match the bed spread. Is this bed all mines? My Mama don't, have to sleep with me. No Henry she don't, it all for you. I set on the bed and my God it felt good it didn't sink like the one my mama and I slept on. Becky, can I stay here all the time?

Oh yes, you can stay as long as you want too.

Wow, Wow! Father came in and (said) son is everything okay? Yes! He gave me a big hug. I knew I was going to like it here. Becky was real nice to me and after a while I started to call her Mom and she loved it. Becky looks like she could be my Mama. After a while I stop thinking about Cherry Etta because I was a white boy and I live in a white neighborhood and I was happy because this is where I belong. Father took me to school and no one ever said anything about me or mean to me and I loved my new school. I was so happy I forgot all about living on Second Street and my black family. One day father came in my room and said Henry I have something to tell you. You going to have a little sister or brother in a few months, would you like that? I guess so. Son I will always love you.

You will always be my little man and I don't want you to ever forget I will always love you and Becky will too. A few months later l had a little sister and they name her Barbara Jean Wilson. She was a cute little baby only so red she looks just like Mom. It's been (2) year since I been with my father. We never talk about Cherry Etta.

The book store father work for was up for sale and father bought it. And we moved to North West 29th Street. The house was bigger, father wanted to have friends over for parties.

I heard father tell Mom he think he made a mistake buying that big house it cost too much to keep it up so he will have to find him another job. He found a job working in the oil fields.

Grandpa Wilson was a very wealthy man in Mississippi he owned the biggest cotton gin there. Father said he didn't want money from Grandpa, he wanted his own money.

Father came home one day and told Mom he just bought some land in the country and one of these days he will build a bigger house for the kids. When Barbara was three years old Mom gave her a birthday party and invited a few of her friend's kids. Father came home just yelling Becky, Becky we rich, we rich. Mom asks him if he was going crazy. He said he just found oil on his land. A few months later we moved again to a bigger house on North 47th and Western. I was so happy because I found me a new friend name Dean Carr. His father owned two oil wells and a car lot down town.

My father and Dean father became friend also. They got together and open a lot of filing station all over town. Father built us one of the biggest houses across sixty third and Pennsylvania Avenue. We lived in the richer neighborhood in town. We were so happy. Dean father build him a home down the street from us. When I became sixteen in 1936 father bought me a new 1936 Ford car for my birthday. I looked out the door and there sit this big black shinning Ford. Father (said) it's your son "Happy Birthday".

Father taught me how to drive. I almost tore the gears out, father said I have to take it easy and slow down. After a few weeks I was driving all over town.

I drove to school every day. Dean father gave him a1936 Chevrolet. One day Dean and I were riding around town and I drove on Second Street. I saw all these black people walking up and down the streets I saw a barber shop, a movie theater. A big church on one corner and a cross the street there was a Hotel. I saw joints and people dancing on the streets people standing talking, I saw restaurants that said barbecue, fried chicken, and hamburgers fried fish. I saw places where you could go in and play pool. I saw people sitting in front of their business on the sidewalk.

I saw women standing on the street corners men driving real fancy cars. I drove slowly because there were kids playing in the streets. I drove down a little ways and people were in their yards and people playing cards under a tree. I came to this house and for some reason I stop in front of it.

Dean (said) what you stopping here for? I don't know. Dean (said) let's get off this street. As we were driving down the street to leave we heard these two men cussing each other and then they started to fight, one man fell to the ground and the other one shot him. Dean was so scared. 'Henry Lee let's get the hell out of here before he shoot us". Why in the hell did you come on this street? Is this the first time you been here?

My daddy knows I'm down here he will kill me. Let's go Henry.

We left and I drove home.

Dean and I went to my room. Dean was really shaking. Man why in the hell you wanted to go down there with all those people? I don't know Dean! Is that your first time there? Yes!

I'll talk to you tomorrow I'm going home. I tried to think why did I go to 2rd Street and stop in front of that house. It seem like I had been there before. I didn't say anything to Mom or father that I had been there. A few days later father came in my room mad. "Henry Lee" what in the hell you doing down there on 2rd street? Dean, Dad told me the two of you were down there and you saw a shooting. Let me tell you one damn thing I better not catch you down there any more I'll take that damn car away from you do you hear me? Yes father! What on earth you doing down there? I don't know I was driving and just end up there. I don't want you in that part of town anymore; you stay in your room the rest of the day.

I didn't understand what the big deal, their only people.

I didn't go back down there anymore, but I did wonder why I wanted to go there. It's been three months since I was on 2rd Street. Basketball season started and I was one of the starters on the team. One night when I was playing I heard someone call my name every time I made a score I look in the stand and I saw this black woman just yelling my name. I wonder who she was she was with this white woman. I thought she was happy we were winning. Then when the white lady son made a point she and the white lady yell so loud. I didn't think any more about it.

After the game I didn't see her.

Father was at my game that night. I never saw that lady again at any of my games.

I was a good student I was on the honor roll and a straight A + student I study real hard because father wanted me to become a lawyer. He helps me a lot studying for law school while I was in middle school and doing the summer when school was out. Father friend James Farmer would let me come in and help him around his office and teach me how to do different things in his law office.

I graduated from high school when I was seventeen I went to college at Oklahoma University my first year; then father wanted me to go to Harvard and I graduate from law school in1945. I work at Farmers Law office until I open my own office.

Dean and I were roommates in college, we graduate together and we open our law office together. I name my law office "Wilson and Carr Law Office". One day 1949 this old black lady came in my office (and said) son can you help me. What can I do for you? Your Mama needs help. No my Mother is find you have me mix up with someone else. I know who you are Henry Lee.

You the lady I saw at my basketball game one night when I was in high school. Yes I am I work for Mrs. Smith and I ask her if she would take me to one of your games I heard how good you were and I wanted to see you.

Who are you? I'm your grandma Cora Jackson.

Ma'am I Henry Lee Wilson and my father is Robert and my mother is Becky Ann Wilson.

Henry Lee you my daughter son your Mama name is Cherry Etta Jackson I help deliver you in this world and help take care of you till you were five years old.

Your daddy bought Cherry, Thomas and me here from Walnut Mississippi. When your daddy got here to Oklahoma he put us down there on 2nd Street and left us. Three months later he came, and took you from your mama and told us to never come for you or see you. I wanted to see you I miss you so much that is why I came to your basketball game and your daddy saw me and told me that if he saw me there anymore he would sent all our black ass back to Mississippi. I never tried to see you anymore. Now I don't care if Robert sends me back home, my daughter needs you. I'm sorry Ma'am I can't help you. Will you help your Mama I don't want her to die? Please help my baby she all I got. I'm sorry Ma'am.

I looked at this old woman as she walk out the door she turn around look at me with tears running down her face. After she left I wonder what in the hell is she talking about? And who in the hell she was, she couldn't be my grandma. My grandpa and grandma is white, the only black people I know are the ones that work for us.

Becky is my mother. When I got home I didn't tell

my father about the old woman because I thought I knew how he felt about black people. He didn't want me around them. I wanted to know what she was talking about. She knew my father and where he came from.

I started to wonder what in the hell is going on because I'm white?

A black woman couldn't be my mother. That lady had to be wrong.

When I got up the next morning Father and Mom was waiting for me to have breakfast with them. Henry Lee you okay? You look tired you didn't sleep well. I'm fine Mom. I have a case I need to check out and I need to fine a lot of answer to and a lot of questions.

What the case about son? Can you talk about it? There was this old black lady came in my office yesterday and she said she need me to help her daughter. I looked at my father and his face turn red and he drop his head. My Mom kept eating. Then my father (said) what did the lady do? I don't know I asked her to leave my office.

Father she said her daughter was going to die if I didn't help her.

Did she tell you her name? No she left crying.

Thank you Mom for breakfast I have to go, I have to be in court at 11:00 am this morning. On my way to court I couldn't get Mrs. Jackson out of my mind and what she said to me she act like she really knew me. After I got out of court I remember the house on 2nd Street and wonder if she lived there. I got in my car and went to see if I could find the house. I saw a man on the street and I ask him did he know a lady name Cora Jackson? He (said) yes she lives in that house right there. I park in front of the house and sit there for a minute. I remember when I was sixteen I stop in front of this house. The house was old and need to be painted there were a few wreck cars park on the side of the house, not much grass in the yard and a big black dog chained near the door. I got out of the car and started to walk to the house, the dog started to bark at me as if he wanted to eat me up. The door open and Cora told the dog to be quite and lay down. Henry Lee I knew you would come I knew in my heart God would send you to me. I knew you would come. Come on in baby have a set. When I walk in I saw a bed in the living room a flower couch and two chairs that didn't match with a small table between them. Over by a window was a table with a lot of pictures on it. Over in the corner were a stove and the house smell like medicine. Cora had a red rag tired around her head and a brown flower dress on with button all the way down the front and brown run over shoes. She was standing there looking at me with tears running down her face. Can I give you a hug son? It's been so long you still look like your daddy. I know you not mean like your daddy. I let her hug me and it felt right. I sit down and said to her, you said I'm your grandson how can that be I'm a white man? My father is white and my mother is white.

You know son sometimes God play tricks on us. She walked over to the table and gave me this picture of my father and this young black girl with her arm around his shoulder. He was sitting down with this little white baby in his arms. I kept looking at this picture and I knew it was my father his lips were the same and he had brown hair and gray eyes. Son your daddy and Cherry Etta were so young when they got together your daddy loved her until we came to Oklahoma City. He found him a wife and broke Cherry heart so bad I couldn't help her. All of a sudden I felt real sick it was because of the medicine smell in the house, I got up to leave when I got to the door there stood this short fat black man with a real mean look on his face. I was a little scare. Cora (said) Thomas this is your grandson. Yes! I know, what you doing here boy? Your daddy, know you here? Thomas, Henry going to help his Mama. Before I had anything to say I ran out the door got in my car and drove off. I went back to my office and my secretory (said) Mr. Wilson your father keep calling for you he want to know where you were and want you to call him as soon as you return. Did he say what he wants? No! If he calls back I don't want to talk to him right now. Is everything alright Mr. Wilson? Cancel all my appointments for the day. I went in my office I just wanted to think what was going on, I wanted to find out about this woman Cherry Etta. I didn't know if to go back to Cora house. I didn't know what to do. My father told me to stay away from black people and I find out he have a baby by a black woman. I got ready to leave to go home and ask father if it was true what this woman said. He walks in the door. Henry Lee why haven't you answer my calls? Father I need to know what is going on. And don't tell me to stay away from them people and not telling me why. I went to see Cora Jackson and I met her and her husband Thomas. She said they were my grandparent. I saw a picture of you and their daughter and she said I was the baby in the picture. How can they be my family? Are they telling the truth? Don't lie to me father. "Yes" Cherry is your mama, we were so young I saw this pretty little black girl and I thought she was the most beautiful little thing I ever saw, I loved your mama and I didn't care what people said or thought about us. She lived on our planation. You know how the people live there. When she told me she was going to have a baby I didn't know what to think or do. When you were born I knew then what to do I wanted you so bad and I knew I would never let you go. I wanted to move to Oklahoma and bring you with me I knew I could see your Mama every time I go back home. Your Mama started to cry because I was bringing you, I felt sorry for her so I bought her with me Her mama and daddy wanted to come to so I bought them because they could help Cherry with you while I work. After we got here I moved them on Second Street I couldn't stay with her, the black people didn't want me on 2nd Street. They were teasing Cherry about me living there. Cherry felt shame of me because of the teasing she got from the people. I found me a place across Robertson Street so I could be near her and to see you when, ever I could. Your Mama started to hung out with people on the street, I didn't think she wanted me anymore, she met a black man and told me to stop coming around, so I met Becky fell in love with her, I told her about you, and I wanted you in my life I miss you so much. Becky told me to get a lawyer and she would help me with you. The day I went to talk to a lawyer Cherry call me and told me you were crying a lot because you miss me and she wanted me to come visit with you. I came and got you because I loved you so much. I told your Mama not to come around you because it would only confuse you. When I bought you home with me Becky fell in love with you and she still love you as if you were her own son. I didn't think you would ever fine out. I'm so sorry son I only wanted to protect you. Son please don't worry about Cherry, don't get mix up with them I'm scare you will get hurt. Son you live a good life none of my friends know Becky is not your mother Becky is your mother. Son I have big dreams for you I want you to run for Senator of Oklahoma. I'll get Cherry a good lawyer, son don't blow things up for yourself. I'll see you later father I need to think I'm going for a drive. My father is right I'll leave thing along I won't go back on Second Street I don't want to be a part of their life I'm a white man no one will ever know. I belong in the white world and not with the black people. When I came back home I walk in my Mom and father look at me I knew he had told her everything me finding out, she was not my Mom. I could tell by the way she looks at me. I just went to my room and sit at my desk and tried to read some papers for my next Court date. All I could do was think about what Cora said. I couldn't sleep couldn't half eat. I knew I had to go back to see Cora. The next day I went back on Second Street. I knock on Cora door she came to the door and started crying (saying) I knew it, thank God I knew you would come back to help your Mama. Tell me about Cherry I don't know anything about her. They got my baby in jail in Derry Oklahoma it's about sixty two miles from here. Well son after your daddy got married, your Mama started hanging out every day on the street I couldn't do nothing with her. She was drinking smoking. She wouldn't listen to nothing I say to her. She would cry saying how much she misses her baby and couldn't ever see him again because your daddy wouldn't let her see you. One day she went to see you. And your daddy had moved. She knew she would never see you again and she felt your daddy no longer cared about her, so she came home with a man name Tommie Ward was a bad man he just got out of jail but she said she love him, he would make her do whatever he wanted to, he had my baby selling her ass to anybody to make money, because he didn't want to work. He came home with her one day and he got smart with her and act like he was going to hit her, I went in my room and I came back with my snub nose thirty eight put it to his head to blow his ass back to where his damn Mama live and she would know where he was at all times. Your Mama told me to put that gun down she love him and I couldn't do that to him she had the nerve to ask me if I lost my damn mind pulling a gun on people. So I told her to get her ass out of here and don't come back she left with him. I didn't like him back in 1935 he shot a man down the street by the Aldridge Theater around 2:30 after noon, the man died. They caught Tommie and he only got three year because it was self-defense, but he had other charger. Your Mama found out she was going to have a baby, she had a little girl she would go visit him two years later she had another one and it was a girl. When he got out they left Oklahoma City going to Colorado but they made it to Derry and stayed because they didn't have money, a year later she had a boy. I could hear Cora talking to me but my mind went back to when I was sixteen Dean and I saw the killing. What is the world will Dean think when I tell him it was my Mama boy, friend that kill that man. Lord what am I getting myself into? Henry Lee, Henry Lee is you listening to me. "Oh yes, yes". You look like you just went out in left field on me. I'm sorry I was just thinking about what you said. Cora I'm sorry I have to go. Henry Lee you don't have a lot of time are you going to help your Mama I don't want my baby to go to prison she got them kids. She is your Mama boy. I had to get out of there. The smell of medicine was making me sick. When I got to the car I didn't know if to run and just keep running. Father wanted me to stay away from black people when I was growing up and now I find out he was in love with a black woman and had a baby by her. When I go home to Mississippi my white family never told me about my black family they are always nice to me they have never call me out of my name or said nothing. I went back to my office Dean was there. Say Henry where you been? What the matter you got that look on your face when we were sixteen and you saw that man get killed on second street, what wrong have you been back down there? Yes you have you saw another killing. Did, you did you? No Dean it's not nothing like that, Well what the hell wrong with you, you know you can tell me anything. Man you don't want to know. You got some woman pregnant you haven't told me about. Oh man your daddy going to kill you. You know how much he want you in the White House. Give the girl some money and take care of that. I can deal with that Dean I wish that was all to it. Damn Henry what have you done? Please Dean it's something I have to do for myself. I'll tell you later, come on let's get the hell out of here I'll buy you a drink I really need one. We went to a bar on Main Street. Dean really wants to know what's wrong with me. I know if I tell Dean, his family will tell him to stay away from me they, don't like black's.

Dean and I been friend ever since we were kids and I don't want to lose him. We went through College and we have our Law Office together. I got drunk and Dean drove me home, Father was waiting for me to come home. Son, have you decide what you want to do about your Mama? I need to know more about Cherry and why she killed that man. I need to talk to her. Father did you know she had more kids? I have two sisters and a brother. I remember when I was sixteen and Dean Dad told you I went to 2nd street and you got so mad at me I put it out of my mind and now it's back. I have to go to Derry and talk to her. Son please leave, it along. I'm sorry father I have to go. The next day I went to Derry Oklahoma. When I got there the court house sit in the middle of down town. Derry is a small nice clean town. I park and went in the Sheriff office. May I help you (the officer said). Yes I would like to see Cherry Etta Jackson. Who are you? I'm her lawyer. You not around here I know all the lawyers here where you from? I'm from Oklahoma City. Well I'll be damn Cherry got money to get a lawyer from the City. Well she have to have a good lawyer to get her ass out of the mess she in. Come on follow me. You want to walk up the stairs or catch the elevator? I'll catch the elevators. When we got upstairs he took me to her cell it was the last one on the right. She was lying down on a bunk with her back turned. The (Office said) Cherry your lawyer is here. Officer, do you have a room where we can talk? No she can't leave this cell. When Cherry Etta turned over and saw me she just sits there and said nothing. I stood there looking at her I was five year old the last time I saw her. 22 years later I see her behind bars. She started to cry. Hello Cherry Etta my name is. I know you Henry Lee my baby. You look just like your daddy. I looked at this little lady with the most sadist eye I ever seen with tears running down her face as if to say everything is going to be alright. Henry Lee do you know you my son did your daddy tell you I'm your Mama? Does he know you here? Yes! I'm so sorry you had to come see me in this place. I wanted to come see you but your daddy wouldn't let me. He said if I came back to see you he would make sure I disappeared, and no one would ever find me so I stayed away from you. I thought about you every day I knew one day you would find me. I always loved you in my heart I had to leave Oklahoma City so I wouldn't cause trouble with your daddy. I found out where he moved and I park across the street and watch you in the yard I just wanted to see you before I left town you lived on 47th street in that big house. Your daddy drove up and saw me. He came to the car and said for me to get the hell away from his house. He said you were fine, he said he was going in the house and call the police on me and for me to never come back to his house. Son you don't know how hard it is for a mother to give up her child, but I knew in my heart I felt it would be better for you. I cried for days when I had to let you go. A year later I came back hoping to see you outside I was going to just drive by and keep going but I found out your daddy moved again. Baby can I just put my arms around you? I just want to feel my baby in my arms. When she hugs me I knew she was my Mama. I could feel the love she had for me. It felt different from the way Mom Becky hug me it's wasn't the same Cherry Etta let go of me I could see the love she had for me. Cherry Etta your mother came to me and said you need my help. I'm a criminal lawyer and I a very good one. I graduate from Harvard I pass the bar the first time I took the test with high honor I work hard to get my law degree early. I came here to help you; I need to know what happen? I need to know about your life what kind of person you are. How do the people here feel about you? I can't tell you everything will be alright for you because you killed a man and I want to know why? You rest today and I'll come back tomorrow. Are you going back to the City? No I want to look around town and talk to some of your friends. Did someone see you shoot the man? Was he your husband? No we just never got around to get married. I had two girls before he, went to prison he serve three years for murder. When he got out we went back together. Why did you shoot him Cherry? He would beat me a lot and I just got tired of it I couldn't take it anymore. I bought a gun and I made up my mind if he hit me again I plan to kill him, that day he was hurting my baby and I had it. Cherry started to cry. Ok

Cherry we will talk later. Henry Lee you have two sister and a brother; I need to get out of here and see about my kids. They all along will you go check on them for me? And let me know if they are alright please they saw me kill Tommy I haven't seen them since I been it here I'm so worried about my kids I don't know what they think of me. I live at 121 Jackson Street. Just tell them you're my lawyer and their brother, and I told you to come by and see how they are doing. Henry Lee, will you get me out of here, and I'll make it up to you one day son. Please just get me out of here. That bastard deserved to die I was protecting me and my kids. You try to get a good night sleep and I'll talk to you tomorrow. When the jailer open, the cell door to let me out I look back at her and she was smiling. The jailer (said) Cherry, I haven't seen you smile like that since you been in here what did you say to her boy? I know you didn't tell her you getting her out of this mess, because her ass is going to prison. There no way she getting out of here? She, going before Judge Reid and he is not the one to play with. He, don't look kind on killers. Yes her ass gone be in for a long time. I just looked at him and (said) have a good day. I walk out of the court house and went to see if I could find Jackson Street. I found Cherry Etta house it was the last house on a dead end street. When I drove up I saw these kids looking out the door. When I got to the door this tall young girl (said) what do you want? Hello my name is Henry Lee, your mother told me to come by and talk to you and to let her know if you kids were doing okay. What is your name? Shelly Ward. May I come in I'm going to help your mother get out of jail. (Shelly, open the door) and I came in. This is my sister Carrie and my brother Harold. Are you going to help my Mama? We scare here by ourselves. Yes Harold I'm going to do my best. Have you kids had anything to eat? Yes but we almost out of food, Shelly can't cook like Mama. Well Carrie, I'll make sure you have enough food until your Mama come home. Shelly can you tell me what happen to your daddy? Were, you home when it happen? "Yes" (Shelly started to cry). If you don't want to talk today I can come back tomorrow. Would you kids like to go to the store with me to buy food? Will you bring us back we not supposed to go with strangers? Yes I promise Carrie I'll bring you back. They got in the car with me and I took them to the store and they got everything they wanted and Shelly got stuff she knew how to cook. I took them back home and help take the food inside. I told them I would come back tomorrow. When I got to the door to leave Shelly (said) Mr. Henry thank you my Mama told me not to open the door for no one but you seem like a nice man. I fell I can trust you and you will help my Mama. Thank, you Shelly. My Mama had to shot my daddy because he was beating us all the time. I'm so scared. Shelly it's late I can come back tomorrow. No I will tell you what happen. I looked around the house and it was almost like Cora house there was a bed in the living room a wood stove in the corner a couch two chairs and a small table. Harold slept in the bed in the living room. Shelly and Carrie had to share a bed room. Cherry Etta room had a bed a chest, night stand and a chair in there. She had a small kitchen with a table and three chairs around it. I felt so bad they live in this small house and not much in it. I lived in a big house with five bed rooms four bathrooms a big kitchen, large dinner room, with eight chairs around the table, a large study with all my law books and full of furniture, living room bigger than their house and a large den full size basement with a bar and everything we wanted in it, three car garage and a swimming pool in the back yard. I had maids and servants I had everything a rich man could own. I never had to live like Cherry Etta and her kids. I sit at the table in the kitchen to write everything Shell would tell me. Carrie and Harold just looked at me and Shelly sit down and started to talk to me. My daddy came home drunk like he always did, he grab me and started kissing me he said I was old enough now for him to teach me to be a woman. He made Harold and Carrie go outside and play and not to come back in until he tells them. He wouldn't let go of me he started to take me in the bed room with him. I told him to stop I didn't want to go with him. I kept begging him I tried to fight him and he slap me real hard I was crying and begging him to please leave me along. He threw me on the bed and pulls his pants down.

Mama came home early from work and walk in the bed room and (said) what in the hell you doing? Take your damn hands off her, she ran over and started beating him and he hit her back. And he, knock her to the floor. She told me to get out and go to my room. She was cussing him and told him she was going to kill him she was sick of his ass, she would kill him before she let him touch me like that. She got up off the floor and started fighting him again and he started kicking her and I ran back in the room to help my Mama and while I was on his back he was trying to get me off and I looked around and I saw Mama standing there with a gun in her hand. She told me to get the hell out of the room now and don't come back. When I left the room I heard gun shots and Daddy came out of the room and went out the door and fell dead in the front yard and Mama went outside with the gun still in her hand and she (said) you black bastard you go to hell where you belong, and she kept pulling the trigger but it just kept clicking she had empty the gun on him. Mr. Henry I was screaming and screaming I was so scared Mama hug, me and told me she was so sorry for what he was trying to do to me. Mama told us to go to Miss Ross house and stay there with her before the police come. Mama was crying and crying and Mr. Henry blood was everywhere. How old are you Shelly? I'm 14. Was that the first time he tried to do that to you? No he tried lots of times when he was drunk and Mama was not at home. I would take Carrie and Harold to

Miss Ross and we would stay until Mama came home. But that day he came come home before we could get out of the house. Did you ever tell your Mama what he was trying to do to you? No because he said he would kill her and they was all ways fighting. He was real mean. She got mad because I never told her before; she said she would have killed his black ass a long time ago if I had told her. That is why I didn't tell her because I knew she would do something crazy and I didn't want her to get in trouble. They would get in fights and she always fight him back and he would leave and sometimes he would be gone for days We were so happy when he was gone and when he come back she would let him. The police came and they were there a long time and they put Mama in the car and took her to jail. We were under the tree with Miss Ross when one of the policeman, came to talk to us. Miss Ross wouldn't let him. She told him we were to scare and for him to wait until we calm down. Miss Ross called Grandma and Grandpa Jackson to come for us and told them what happen. Grandma Cora and Grandpa Jackson came to take us back with them but we didn't want to leave Mama we wanted to be home when she get out of jail. I told Grandma I would keep the door lock. Grandma Cora said she had to go back to Oklahoma City because she knew someone that could help Mama. Grandpa said he had to go back because someone would break in his house and steal everything he had. They ask Miss Ross to keep an eye on us. Miss Ross is here every day she will take care of us. Shelly can I ask you to tell me something about your father? I can't believe a father would want to hurt you like that. What kind of man was he? He was a bad man, he was always doing things he had a girlfriend he would go to Ponca City to be with her for days and when he come back home Mama would let him come back. She said she wanted to keep her family together and he was the father of her kids. I never could understand what that mean, he was always hurting us, I thought she was a little scare of him. Tell me everything about him. I need to know so I can help your mother, if you don't want to talk about him right now we can talk later. Mr. Henry I'll tell you because I miss my Mama we need her here with us. I always take care of Carrie and Harold because Mama had to work. I always hated my daddy because he was always mean to us, he made us do everything for him he would say go get me this, get me that, bring me this, bring me that. He was okay when he wasn't drinking he would do so many crazy things. I remember one day when he was drunk the lady across the street dog didn't like him and her, dog ran out and bit him on the leg, he grab the dog and broke his neck and threw the dog in the lady yard and walk in the house as if he didn't do anything. Police came and talk to him, and he told them the dog bit him and he was scare the dog was going to bite him again, so he did it in self-defense. The police didn't do anything to him. One day he went over to one of his friend's house and it was snowing so hard, the ground was cover with snow, he came home kick open our front door and came in and I couldn't help but laugh and laugh, because he only had on some white socks and some long handle underwear, and he was cover with snow all you could see was a snow man with a black face. I couldn't stop laughing, he pick up one of Harold boots and threw it at me. Mama asked him what in the hell was wrong with him where in the hell was his clothes. We later found out that his friend came home early and found him in bed with his wife and they got in a fight and his friend wouldn't give him his clothes and he had to walk home in all that snow. (Carrie and Harold started laughing.) Carrie said Mr Henry that is the only time he ever made us laughs. Shelly, tell Mr. Henry what he did when he worked at Mr. Wakens grocery store. Mr Wakens came and ask him if he could come to his store and mop and wax the floor once a week. Mama was so happy she told Mr. Wakens yes, daddy will take the job, so when daddy went to work Mr. Wakens told him that he was going to lock him up in the store so he wouldn't steal nothing. Daddy put on some big pants and a big coat because it was winter time. When he got in the store Mr. Wakens took his coat and hung it up in his office, and he lock the door so he wouldn't put anything in his coat pocket he told Daddy he would be back in an hour to let him out to go home. When Mr Wakens came back (he said)

Tommy empty your pockets. Daddy did and there was nothing in them, he gave Daddy his coat and told him you can come back because you not a thief. When Daddy came home he pull off his pants and man we were shock, Daddy had all kind of lunch meat tape down his leg with masking tape in the inside of his of his legs he had pork chops, beef roast, and bacon. We had meat for days. Every week he would bring meat home. One day he was half drunk and he didn't tape the meat good to his leg and the meat started to fall out from under his pants Mr. Wakens was so mad he made him take all the meat out of his pants and took Daddy to the door and kick him out of his store and told him never come back. So we had to go to Standby grocery down by the train station. Mr Stanly like Mama he would let her have food on credit and some time on her days off she would help him stock up for the next day, daddy went to the store one night and caught them kissing daddy was so mad he hit Mr Stanly and grab Mama by her hair and pull her out the store and told her he don't know why she love white men, he made her quit working there. Miss Ross and Mrs Taylor buy our food for us when they go to the stores. Daddy never works again because everyone heard about what he did. He was a very mean man and he was always doing something wrong when he was drinking, Down the street a man name Mr Joe Cootie got mad at him because he though daddy was messing with his wife, They started cussing each other and next thing they were fighting, Daddy hit him so hard Mr Cootie fell and broke his hip, Police came out and took daddy to jail he stay in jail for three days and they let him go because Mr Cootie didn't press chargers on him. When Joe Cootie lhip got well he had to walk with a limp every time he took a few step he had to stop and shake his booty, so all of the people in Derry would say here come Joe Cootie with the timberline bootie it was sad that he had to walk like that for the rest of his life, Daddy act like he didn't care. Daddy loved women; we tried to get Mama to leave him because he was always doing something wrong when he was drunk. We think Mama was scare of him; they would cuss and fight all the time. Mr Henry he was always doing something when he was drunk they said he changed when he killed a man and had to go to prison. I'm glad he is gone forever he will never hurt Mama or anyone else any more. I felt so sad and bad for my sisters and brother, I couldn't image what else they had to go through. I told them that I'm going to do everything I can to bring their Mama home. I looked over at Harold and I could see tears running down his face I ask him what was wrong? He said Mr. Henry I don't want my daddy to ever come back he beat me so bad. One day Carrie and I was playing outside and, I push her she fell and hit her head on a big rock and she look like she was dead, Shelly told him to come help and he came out side and try to get Carrie to open her eyes and she wouldn't. He got the water hose and just shot water all over Carrie she wake up just holing.

After that he got a board and put my head between his legs and my butt was up and he beat me with that board until I couldn't cry anymore and it made him mad because I stop crying, my butt was so numb I couldn't feel it. Mama came home and Shelly told her what he did, and she didn't say anything she went in her room and came out with that gun and put it to his head and told him she should kill him. He beg and beg her not to kill him. She told him if he ever put his hand on any one of us again she would kill him. He put his hands on Shelly and that is when she killed him. I felt so sad for Harold I ask him if I could give him a hug? He ran to me and hugs me. I said to my brother and sisters that as long as I live I will never let anyone hurt them again. Shelly said thank you Mr. Henry. Shelly would you and the kids like to go out and eat dinner and spend a night in a motel I'll get you guys a room next to me. No thank you Mr. Henry we will stay right here till Mama come home. Thank you very much for the food. When Mama comes home I'll tell her to pay you. No Shelly I'm glad I could do it for you. When I come back I'll bring your Mama with me. You lock the door and don't let anyone in. I looked at my brother and sisters I wanted to put my arms around them and say: I'm your brother and I'm taking you home with me. I knew they wouldn't believe me because I'm a white man. I got in the car and drove half way down the street, near the street I saw a lady sitting under a tree I got out and said good evening, how are you? Oh I'm fine just setting here under this here shade tree trying to keep cool, it's too hot in my house, I don't have a fan they cost too much money. I like sitting here under this tree because I can see everybody up and down this street and everybody that pass by. Sometimes they stop and talk to me like you. I just saw you going in Cherry Etta house and coming back with some bags of grocery. You taking her kids away from her and putting them in an orphan home? No Ma'am I'm a lawyer from Oklahoma City Cherry Etta mother ask me to help her daughter. Do you know Cherry Etta? "Yes I do" Can you tell me anything about her? What kind of person she is? Is she a good mother to her kids? Yes I can, she is a good Mama, she work two jobs so she can take care of her kids, that no good ass man she got she should have killed his ass the first day she met him. He don't work, I would have put his ass out the first time he put his hands on me. He was always fighting that girl and them, poor kids. That girl took a lot of shit off his lazy ass. She was only protecting herself and her kids. Shelly, said when her Mama go to work he was always talking crazy to her and she was scare of him. She said he never rape, her but she was scare that one day he might. She, ask me not to tell her Mama because she didn't want to start no trouble. So since he hasn't rape, her I kept my mouth close so she could tell me everything that went on in that house. I knew that it would be a matter of time he would try. The day came, the day Cherry Etta shot his ass. Shelly is a pretty girl and a good girl her mama leave her with them kids while she works. You know Shelly is only 14 years old. When the kids catch the bus to go across town to Blaine School, he would just be bringing his ass home from being out all night long over to Larry Jones house playing dominoes. Larry have all kind of women in and out of his house that's why he was over to Larry house all night and then come home sleep all day. When the kids come home he make Shelly cook for him. Those poor kids were scare of him. You put me on that stand and I can get Cherry Etta to walk out that court room. When I get through telling those white folks what I know about his sorry ass and how he did her and those poor kids, they will be walking out of that court room saying they would have killed his ass themselves. You just put me on that stand. What did you say your name was? I didn't, but its Ethel Ross and I been here in Derry all my life. And I know everything that goes on in this town. Everybody see me under this tree they stop by and tell everything even the white folks. Thank you Miss. Ross for helping Cherry Etta and her kids. You put me on that stand and I'll help her some more. Miss. Ross I would like for you to be on Cherry Etta side will you not tell anyone you talk to me. I will be back and take you to court with me. Yes son I'll go with you Cherry Etta is a good girl, go down there and get her out so she can be with her kids, the kids don't need to be down there by themselves. I see some of those bad ass boys going down there and Shelly sit outside with them but you don't know how long that will last. Go on get that girl out I'll be the best damn witness you ever had. Now what did you say your name was? Henry Wilson. Henry I got money and I own this house so if you need more money to help Cherry I'll give it to you. Thank you Miss Ross I'll do that. I'll be in touch with you. I went back down town and I saw a bus station, and they serve food, I went in set down at a table. The waitress came over and I order hamburger, coke and fries. While I was setting there I started to write down what I wanted to say to the Judge to get Cherry Etta out on bond. I heard these white people talking at the next table about Cherry Etta. One man said I think Cherry should get the death penalty because if she get by with it all these damn women round here will try to kill all us men. We need to stick together. Floyd you can't think like that she may have snapped. Snapped my ass she knew what she was doing. Cherry is a hard worker. She works for the Taylor family and they love her. I don't give a rat's ass how much they love her, her ass need to go to prison. I don't want these color folks killing people around here and thinking they, going to get by with it. Floyd, eat your food so we can be home when the kids get there. After I listen to them talk I didn't know how all the people in Derry felt about Cherry Etta. I sit there and wonder if I should get in my car and drive back to Oklahoma City and let someone else take her case. I didn't know if she had a chance after listening to what Floyd said. I thought about how nice Shelly was and I told her I would help her mother. Then I thought about Carrie and Harold how much they had gone through. I promise Miss Ross. The waitress came to bring my bill. She said I haven't seen you around here are you passing through? No I'm here representing Cherry Etta Jackson. Do you know her? Yes she uses to work here for me cooking and cleaning after we close, I had to let her go. Why? That man of hers kept hanging around here when she was at work. My customers didn't like him to much he was always bossing Cherry and saying she was meeting men when they got off the bus at night. Something was wrong with him I didn't like it when he was always around, he, drink a lot and I thought he was a little crazy. I never could see what Cherry saw in him, He was very lazy. I sure hope you have good luck with Cherry she gone really need it. I decided to go back to the court house to see if the Judge was still there and to see if I could meet him and try to get Cherry out of jail. I found his office and had to wait a long time because I didn't have an appointment with him. I was getting ready to leave to find me a room for the night when he told me to come in his office. I could smell liquor on him, he had been drinking. What can I do for you son? I'm Cherry Etta Jackson lawyer and I want to get her out on bond.

Are you crazy that woman killed an unarm man and you want me to let her go free. Judge she have three young kids home along, she need to be home with her kids. Her ass should have thought about that when she killed their daddy. Judge what can I say or do to change your mind? You know Judge sometimes lawyer need a drink to calm his nerves. Yes son you right, pour you a drink and me one to. Son you can't tell no one we in here drinking. Oh no Judge. The Judge and I drank and talked about Cherry Etta. He said she was a good mother and she was a dear friend of one of his friends. He knew she needed to be home with those girls. (He said) he knew Tommy Ward and he didn't like him but he had to go by the law. We had a few more drinks and I told him I had to leave. You know son I think I like you. What did you say your name was? Henry Wilson. Henry let me call my court clerk in here. Joyce, come in my office now. When Joyce came in he told her to get the court room ready for 9:30 the next morning and have Cherry Etta Jackson record file ready for him and to call Kevin and tell him. Judge (she said) I can't do it today I have other case to do before hers. I'm the damn judge and you do as I say I want Cherry Etta Jackson before me in the morning I'm setting bail for her if you can't have it ready by morning you find someone who can now get the hell out of here. Yes Judge! Henry I' going to set bail for Cherry Etta and I want you to keep an eye on her and I want you to make sure she show up for her court date. I'll have everything ready for you in the morning. Thank you Judge you won't be sorry. I'm holding you responsible for her. Judge I need to go see her. I'll get the jailer to take you to her cell. When Cherry Etta look, up and saw me. Baby what happen? Did you come back to get me out of here? Did you see my kids? Are they alright? Cherry Etta I'm coming back to get you out in the morning. Oh thank you God, Thank you God. Cherry Etta I need you to promise me something. I'll promise you anything just get, me out of here. Keep your mouth close about me being your son and not tell your kids if someone find out they may take me off your case and you will have to get another lawyer and you may in up in prison. Yes I can I promise you just get me out of here. I'll see you tomorrow. I left and found me a room and went back to the bus station the next morning to get me something to eat. On my way back to my room I saw a dress shop on the north side of the court house call Zebra, I went in and got me a suite and everything I need I didn't bring clothes with me because I didn't plan to spend the night. When I got to the counter with everything the man (said) are you going to a wedding or funeral? No I'm going to court. Oh hope it's nothing bad. I'm going to help Cherry Etta Jackson. Why are you going to help her, you know her. I'm her lawyer. "You what" why you a white man can she afford you? I looked at him and paid for my things and walk out. When I got to my room I use the pay phone outside to call father and let him know what was going on and I ask him if he could bring enough money to get Cherry Etta out of jail. The next morning I went back to the jail to tell Cherry Etta that father will bring the money. It will only be a few hours as soon as father can bring the money. (Cherry Etta said) I don't want your damn daddy doing nothing for me he can keep his damn money I just stay in jail before I ask him to do anything for me. The next morning I went to court to get Cherry out on bail. All rise. We stood up and the Judge came in. He (said) we here to set bail for Cherry Etta Jackson. I set bond at one 500.00 hundred dollars. Cherry Etta jump up and said I ain't got that kind of money. Order, Oder calm your prison down or I'll change my mind and lock her back up. Cherry sit back down I told you to keep your mouth close and let me do the talking you say one more word I'll walk out of here and leave you here. I'm sorry Henry Lee. I 'm sorry Judge there will not be another outburst. Judge Reid (said) Cherry Etta Jackson will remain in jail until her bond is paid. I didn't have that much money on me. Cherry was mad as hell. I decide to go talk to Miss Ross to see if she had any cash I told her I need 400, hundred dollars. (She said) Come on take me down to that court house so we can get that girl out. What in the hell wrong with Joe setting her bond so high he done lost his damn mind. When we got back to the court house Miss Rose said I need to see Joe. Yes Miss Ross go, on in. You wait out here Henry I'll be back. I don't know what Miss Ross said but five minutes later she (said) come on and make that check to the court clerk. Are you sure Miss Ross? "Yes" sure as a heart attack. After I paid the clerk they bought Cherry Etta down. Henry Lee where you get the money? Don't worry I'm taking you home to your kids. Thank, you baby. I went to get Miss Ross. Cherry (said) Ethel what you doing here did you give Henry the money to get me out? No he paid every penny. I just came with him. Thank both of you I'll pay you back one day. I can't wait to get to my kids. I call father back and told him I didn't need him to come he said he was taking his time to come because she need to keep her ass in jail to learn a lesson. When I drove up in Cherry Etta yard, the kids ran out the door and grab their Mama they were so happy. Shelly (said) Mr. Henry thank you: you said you would bring her home. I will pay you back as soon as I get a job. Thank you so much. You welcome Shelly we still have a long ways to go you have to help keep your Mama in line until we go back to court. Henry Lee will you come in and let me cook something for you so we can talk. No Cherry I have to get back to the City so I can work on your case I only have a few weeks. You just remember the promise you made me. I will Henry. Cherry Etta began to cry and came over to me and whisper in my ear. I love you son you are so handsome I will see you in a few weeks. I drove off and they were all waving good bye I made it back home and was glad to be home. Mom (said) son did everything go alright?

Yes Mom I kissed her and told her how much I loved her. Where is Father? He is out by the pool. Hi, Father I'm home. Hi son what happen? I told him what Derry was like and the people I met. Henry did you get your Mama out of jail? Or did you leave her so someone else could help her. Why don't you let Dean help her? Have you told Dean she your Mama? No I'm' not ready to tell him or any of my friends or yours, maybe someday but not right now. I love the life I live. I don't want to be an embarrassment to your friends. Father jump up and (said) son I love you and you will not be an embarrassment to me I'm very proud of you. I never want to see you hurt that is the only reason I try to keep thing from you. Son I loved your Mama things just didn't work out like I wanted to. Your Mama was so young; after I found out she was running around on me I had to let her go, what do you think of her? I felt sorry for her and her kids they have nothing, they are so poor. Son, they have each other and that mean a lot to have the love of each other. I know the kids are happy you help get their mother home with them. After talking to father I was tired I went to my room took a shower and got in bed, when I heard a knock on my door it was Mom with a snack tray in her hand. Hey Mom what you got there? I though you would like a little snack before you go to sleep. Thank you. What do you think of your Mama? I really don't know right now. I have two sisters and a brother I feel sorry for them. Son help your mother I know you will do what your heart tell you to do we raise you to be a good man and stand up for all the thing right that you believe in, you are a man now and only you can make your own decision. Sometimes we don't always know what's best, but you have to search your heart son, and do what is best for you. Whatever you want to do I will stand beside you and I will always be here for you. Father, want me to stay away from them. Your father love you so much he fell you may be hurt. Son you have to pray and ask God to help you do the right thing. Thank you Mom I love you so much. No one can ever take away the love I have for you in my heart. Good night son. Good night Mom. I laid there in bed thinking about what father wanted me to do, and I thought about Cherry Etta and her kids. What should I do, give her case to Dean? The next few weeks came so fast it was time for Cherry Etta trial. I went back to Derry and went to Cherry Etta house to get her and take her to court. I knock and knock and no one was home. I hope she and the kids were already at the court house. I was going by Miss Ross house and she was sitting under the tree. I stop and she said she saw Cherry Etta leaving real fast and it was over an hour and she haven't come back home. Do you know where she went too? No she, pass by and didn't stop. Maybe she is at the court house. I have to go Miss Ross, Wait till I get my purse I'm going with you. When Miss Ross and I got in the court room I didn't see Cherry Etta or her kids. I didn't know what to do or say to the Judge. He was nice to let her out on bond and I be damn she haven't show up. The court room was full and so much talking. Why in the hell I didn't I listen to father? The court Attorney was already there to make sure he found her guilty and she doesn't have her ass here. I sit at my table to think what to tell the Judge why she wasn't there. All rises The Judge comes in and the bailiff said you may be seated. I sit down and just as the Judge was ready to ask me where was Cherry Etta I felt someone tap me on my shoulder and say do I sit here next to you? Where have you been I was worried you weren't going to show up? I wasn't I was on my way to Oklahoma City because I know they gone fine me guilty. Shelly made me come back she said you told her that you would help me, you got me out before and she believe you can do it again she said she told you she was praying for you every day. The Judge called the State. The attorney got up and said the state is here to prove on May, 4, 1946 Cherry Etta Jackson murders her boyfriend in cold blood and we will prove she is guilty. State calls your first witness. The State calls Joann Brown. (She was sworn in) Mrs. Brown do you know the plaintiff Yes! How long have you know her? About eight years. I live across the street from her. Can you tell the court what you saw at Cherry Etta Jackson house? I was outside and I heard gun shots and then Tommy came out the door and fell down in the yard and Cherry came out with a gum in her hand. I ran over and ask Cherry what happen and she didn't say anything she drop the gun and sit down on the porch and waited for the police to come. Two more witness said about the same thing as Joann. Judge I have no more questions. Councilor you have question for the witnesses. No! Call your witnesses. Judge I call Shelly Ward. Shelly do you swear to tell the truth and nothing but the truth so help you God. Yes! Shelly can you tell me how old you are? I'm 14

Is Cherry Etta Jackson your mother? "Yes" Do you love your mother? Yes! Will you say anything to save your mother? Yes I will tell the truth. Did you love your father? No!! Can you tell me why you don't love your father? Because, he was always trying to get me to, go to bed with him when Mama wasn't home. Did you tell your Mama? No because he said he would kill me and her and I was scare of him. He would always beat on Mama and us kids. I'm glad he is dead I'm glad, glad I want have to ever see him again. Shelly started to cry so hard the Judge ask her if she would like to step down and get herself together. Call your next witness. I call Ethel Ross to the stand. Will you state your name? My name is Ethel May Ross. Do you swear to tell the truth and nothing but the truth so help you God? I do. Ethel do you know Cherry Etta Jackson? Yes I do. How long have you known her? I met her when she moved to Derry (eight years ago) she live down the street from me. Miss Ross the day Tommy Ward was killed did you see anything Yes I did and you listen to me before you ask me any more question. I want to say something and I want all you folks in here listen to me. (DA said I Object). Miss Ross you can only say yes or no. What I have to say is yes and all you going to listen to me and I am not getting down until I say what I have to say. (the State said we object) you answer yes or no. Miss Ross looked at the Judge (and said) Joe you know me and you go way back you don't want to make me mad. Judge Reid told the D A to sit down and let her talk. Miss Ross looked at the D A (and said) Kevin, you know I know everything that go on in this town some of these white folks come and sit with me under my tree and tell me everything. The D A just shook his head. The people in the court room started laughing. Order, order in my courtroom. Ethel, say what you have to say and get down. Thank you Judge. Ethel (started to talk) I went to her house and I welcome her and her kids to Derry and I told her who I was. Cherry Etta is nice to me we get along fine when she had Harold I help bring him in this world. That damn pair pants was nowhere to be found. Ethel, watch your language and you have to call people by their names for the record. Ok Joe. Ethel you have to call me Judge Reid you're in my court. Oh well, that Tommy Ward didn't come home for two days after Harold was born. I went to Cherry Etta house every day to take care of her and them kids. We didn't know where he was. When he came home he smelled like a damn Donkey running for his life, boy did he stink.

(The people started laughing). Ethel I'm not going to tell you no more you keep that up and you have to get off the stand. (The D A kept shaking his head and said nothing). I looked at the jury and they wanted to hear what Ethel had to say. Ethel (said) can I keep talking Judge? Yes Ethel but watch your mouth. Tommy came home and came in the bed room and told Cherry to get her ass out of that bed and cook him something to eat. She told him she just had the baby and she couldn't get out of bed. I wasn't scare of him like she was I told him to fix his on damn food or go back where he came from and eat, because Cherry wasn't cooking his ass no food and take his stinky ass in there and take a bath. He told me to get my noise ass out of his house and never come back. Before, he, do something else bad to me again. And I wanted to know what he, mean bad to me again, he wouldn't say anything. I told him you bastard if you ever try to hurt me you will never see the light of day again I can't prove you had something to do with my son death If I find out you did you better watch out for me, because somebody might find nothing but your ass tied on the train track after the train run over you. He got quite and went in the other room. He knew not to mess with me. The D A, got up and said Ethel all I want you to do is tell me what you saw the day Tommy Ward was killed if you don't know nothing get down. Ethel looked at him and (said) Kevin if you interrupt me one more time I will call Lulu and let her know what you up to you know I know. You sit down and let me finish I be done in a minute. You need to let me hurry and tell you what I know. Henry where was I? You were telling us about Tommy Ward. Oh yes I told him he may scare Cherry but I am not the one I told him that I would beat his black ass before he could draw his hand back to hit me. And if I couldn't beat him I would pull my 45 out and shoot the shit out of him. I know it would catch his ass running from me. The court room started laughing. Tommy was always beating on that little girl, he better be glad I wasn't his wife when he put his hand on me the first time his Mama would have known where he was at all time and where to find him whenever she wanted to know where he was. The kids come up to my house always calling the police on him. They came out and took him to jail and a few days later here he come back. That poor girl had to go back to work at the bus station when her baby was three week old. Shelly had to keep that baby and I would go help her because he said he didn't do babies. Lord, Lord. Ethel drops her head and said nothing for a few seconds. The court room got so quite you couldn't even hear a baby cry. Then she (said) you know Kevin one day I was sitting out there under my tree and I saw Cherry come running out of the house and down the street to my house and there he come right behind her just cussing and calling her all kinds of names. Them, poor kids was just crying and begging him to leave their Mama along. I got up and went in the house and I came back with my 45 in my hand. The police was call out there so much they half come out so that day I was ready for him,

The, police would never have to come back for him. The neighbors stop trying to help her because Cherry kept letting him come back. She said he was the father of her kids and she didn't want them to be without a father and she once care about him. Ethel stop (again) and you could see her eyes was full of water. Ethel looked at the jury and the tears stated to run down her face. Ethel was seventy eight years old and she, look as if she wasn't scare of anyone not even when she was young. Cherry Etta started to cry and the jury looked so sad. Floyd looked as if he didn't give a damn. Ethel kept sitting there and Judge Reid said in a very kind voice Ethel you need to rest. No Joe let me tell my last story and I'll get down. When Cherry ran out that house she was running to me and Tommy pick up a rake in the yard and that dirty bastard was trying to kill her with that rake. When Cherry ran to me that bastard drew that rake to hit her and I stood in front of her with my 45pistol, and I put it in his face and told him to hit me so I could blow his ass all the way back down that street because today was the day he was going to go make a home with old Satan. I shot in the air that bastard drop that rake and fell to the ground he thought I had shot him. He got up and I told him next time I won't miss I shot again and Cherry told me he wasn't worth it. His black ass took out running and I swore I saw dust behind him. Somebody call the police and I heard them coming I gave Shelly the gun and told her to take and hide it out back she ran down the alley and took it home with her. The police drove up and said what's going on here we got a call that someone was shot. Ethel what going on here (they said). I told them that Tommy and Cherry was at it again and he took off running. They ask me if he had a gun and I said I didn't know. They jumped in the car after him. I know it was wrong to give Shelly that gun with her being a kid but at the time I wasn't thinking about her being a kid. I'm really sorry for that. (Shelly shouted out) I'm not sorry you shot in the air you should have hit him. The court room started to clap their hands. Kevin (said) Ethel you know you in trouble for what you just confess to in this court room. Kevin, sit your ass down and you can deal with me later. Judge, have the bailiff take her down I want her arrested now. The people, was getting mad at Kevin. The Judge said order, order. Someone said let her finish what she got to say we want to know. Go head Ethel I want to know too. Well Judge by the time they caught up with his ass he was running so fast he didn't stop until he was cross town and it only took him ten minutes. The Judge wanted to laugh. The court, room just laugh and Kevin was still shaking his head. The police found Tommy at Larry Jones house and that time they kept him in jail for three months for his own safety. While he was in jail everything was going well for Cherry and the kids they were so happy. The neighborhood was so quite without him there, we sure didn't miss his ass. Well he got out of jail and do you know that bastard told Cherry Etta he had changed being in jail. He had time to think about what he was doing to her and the kids. He, promise her he would change. He told her how much he missed her. She let him moved back in and it was only a week he was back drinking. I told her not to listen to him he was lying to her, but she loved him. That day she came home early, when she got home that was the day he was trying to get her baby in bed with him that baby was crying and trying to get away from him. He had already pulled her clothes off. When Cherry walk, in and saw what he was trying to do to her baby. Cherry started to beat on him and that bastard had the nerve to start beating on her. That girl got tired of him beating on her and her kids and taking her money and staying out all night coming home when he wanted. Something was wrong with his sick ass. That drinking drove him crazy. Ethel was still looking at the jury and tears still running down her face. Ethel was it your gun that Cherry used to shoot Tommy? No someone gave Cherry that gun years ago. She never wanted to use it on him until she walk in and that dirty bastard was going to rape her baby. I thank, she just snap and was tired of him mistreating them. I looked at the jury and I could see tears running down their faces and I knew Ethel had won my case for me. Miss Ross, are you through? No I want to say one more thing Cherry is guilty for killing Tommy; she did it to save her life and the life of her kids because one day he may have killed her or one of them kids. I know a lot of you are going through the same thing; you just don't have the courage to stand up for your selves. Isn't that right Kevin? Judge I have no more question for Miss Ross. Do, the State have any question for this witness? No your Honor. State rest its case. You may step down Ethel. Thank you Miss Ross. The Judge told the jury to take their time and come back with a verdict. (It was an all-white jury). Court dismiss until the jury return. When they left some of them look like they felt sorry for Cherry Etta. I was hoping they find Cherry Etta not guilty but you can't always tell what a jury may think. Ethel put a lot on their mind. Hour had gone by and the jury was still out Cherry was worried she thought if it took them that long they would find her guilty. Henry when I go to prison will you go by and help Mama with my kids some times. Make sure they go back home with Mama and Daddy. Another hour pass and I was getting nerves. Thomas, hug Cherry and told her they would make sure the kids would be alright. Cherry hug her kids and told them how much she loved them and please, listen to their grandma. None of Tommy's family was there. Before I left Oklahoma City I went by and told Tommy mother about the trial. And she said she wouldn't come because she lost her son to the streets when he was fifteen years old and she knew she wouldn't get him back. He was in and out of jail all his life. She had five other children she had to worry about them. When Tommy killed that man on 2nd Street he was never the same. After he moved to Derry she never saw him again. She felt sorry for Cherry and her kids she hope someday she could one day see her grandkids, (she said) whatever they do to Cherry will be alright with her. Judge Reid came back in the court room and then the jury. Have you reached a verdict? Yes Judge. Will you read the verdict? Floyd stood up and said we the jury fine Cherry Etta Jackson not guilty we fine self-defense. The court room was so loud everyone was happy Cherry was found not guilty. Judge Reid (said) order, order. I like to say something to Cherry Etta, you were found not guilty it is still not right to take a life, no matter who it is. I do not want to see you in my court room again for taking anyone life. I pray you and your kids will make it in life. I would like to tell Shelly Ward, honey I want you to know that all men are not like your daddy was to you and your family. Your daddy was a very sick man and I hope one day you can find it in your heart to forgive him and I pray you will have a good life. Cherry Etta Jackson you are free to go, court dismiss. Shelly (said) thank you for saving our Mama. I didn't save your Mama, Miss Ross did. They all hug Ethel. Miss Ross you made my job easy. We left the court room, and I told them all it was nice to meet all of them. Cherry ask me if I could follow her home, she and the kids got in the car together and Ethel rode with me, I drop Ethel off and went to say good bye to Cherry Etta and her kids. I told them I had to get back to Oklahoma City and I had to go back to the court house. I was leaving when Cherry Etta (said) Henry you said I could tell the kids who you were after the trial. I want to tell them now. Kid's Henry is your brother. Shelly (said) "brother what you mean brother" This is a white man I don't understand. Mama did something happen to you while you were in jail. No Shelly! Henry Lee is my son his father is white. Shelly (said) I don't believe this. Well believe it. Did you know Mama is your Mama? No I just found out a few weeks ago when Cora came to me and ask me to help your Mama. Why didn't you tell us when you first came to the house? Shelly I didn't know how you would take it. Mama how come you never told us about him? Your daddy didn't want me to because you all wouldn't understand I plan to tell you one day. (Harold said) Why are you so old? You're older then Shelly. I'm sorry Cherry I have to go. I got in the car and drove off. I stop by Miss Ross and thank her again for her help in court. I told her I wish I could have her in all my cases. Hope to see you again Miss Ross. Don't worry son you will believe me you will. Good bye Miss Ross. went back to the court house to see if Judge Reid was still there. He was getting ready to leave and I could still smell liquid on him. Judge I want to thank you for letting Miss Ross speak at Cherry Etta trial. Well if I didn't let Ethel speak her mind I would never have heard the last of it. Ethel and I have been in love ever since we were young. Ethel haven't work a day in her life I been taking care of her for over fifty five years and I still love her. Everybody here knows about it they just look over it and talk about us whenever they want to but I don't give a damn and Ethel don't either. I met Ethel when she was sixteen. My wife knew about it she didn't like it but I couldn't stay away from Ethel. My wife couldn't have kids, and Ethel had a son for me. When he got 8 years old he was playing outside and when Ethel went out to call him in she couldn't find him so she went to Cherry house to see if he was there because sometimes he would go down there to play with Cherry kid's. No one was home so she thought he may have gone to town with Cherry and her kids. When Cherry came home she said she haven't see him. Ethel called me and I went to help look for him. We call the police and they help, going to everyone house looking around the houses and talking to people and no one saw him. Everybody in town was helping look for him. I went down to the low water bridge to see if he was there I walk up and down that stream under that bridge and I found nothing. The next day my wife brother found his body right where I looked. I though he may have killed him and put his body there when no one saw him because no one was looking in white neighborhood. He swore to me he had nothing to do with my son death I could tell if he was lying to me. He always hated that I had a baby by Ethel and his sister stayed with me. I know his body was not there when I went there. Ethel almost lost her mind when our son was found dead. They said he fell in the water and drown and that was that. Joann Brown said she saw Bobby at Cherry Etta house when she was leaving going to town. Cherry and the kids wasn't, home but Tommy was. We looked all around that house to see if we could see anything. Ethel always thought that Tommy had something to do with killing our son that is why Ethel hated him so much. I believe Ethel sit under that tree so she can see everything that go on. Ethel always wanted to just find a way that she could kill him. That is why I didn't say too much to Ethel when she was telling everything he did to Cherry Etta. Tommy said he didn't see my son. I always felt he was lying but I couldn't prove it. He never like, Ethel because she was always taking up for Cherry and the kids. Ethel said Tommy was always mad at Cherry because she had a baby by a white man and it wasn't his first child by her that was one of the reason he would beat her. He hated white men. He knew I was Bobby father and he didn't like Ethel. I was already a lawyer so I work hard to become a Judge so that I could send every murder to prison. The reason why I let Ethel, talk at Cherry trial because I knew she believed he killed our son we couldn't prove it. When I heard Cherry killed his ass I was happy. I had to go by the law for Cherry but if they had found her guilty I had already found away where I could come up with finding that she did it in self-defense. I loved my son by Ethel he was the only kid I ever had. That is the reason I take a little drink I just can't get over where my son was, and then the next day he was found where I had been looking and he was not there. Now that the killer of my son is dead I can stop drinking and I think I may retire. After talking to Judge Reid I felt so sorry for him I wanted to tell him that I was Cherry Etta white son. But I shook his hand and told him I would be back to see him. You do that son for some reason I like you the first time I met you. I'm going to be alright now because God have taken care of everything for me. I can stop drinking, my wife died two years ago I might ask old Ethel to marry me. Good luck to you son. I got in my car to leave I thought I should go back and tell Cherry Etta and the kids good bye. When I drove up she came to the door. Henry Lee what's wrong? Nothing I forgot to say goodbye. We are getting ready to go to Raleigh place to celebrate my home coming. Please come with us it's the best soul food in town. What is soul food? I always ate sea food in Mississippi. You mean you never ate good food. I went with them and boy they had me eating food I never ate before, Cherry Etta order me some collard greens, pig feet, even neck bones cream potato with cheese on top, corn bread. I like the food it was so different for me. Cherry said I had to eat a hamburger they were the best in town. I told her I would take it home with me. It felt real nice to be with my other family. Then it was time for me to go back home. Cora hug me and (said) son I knew you could save my baby. I want to thank you, how much do we owe you? Don't worry Cora everything is on me. They all hug me and I told them all good bye and it was nice meeting them. I got in my car and drove back to Oklahoma City. I went to my office, I was there for a while when I kept smelling that hamburger I had to take a bite, man it was grease and the best burger I ever ate I wanted to go back and buy another. Dean walked in. I heard you won your case in Derry. Yes I did. Was it a hard case? No Dean but I want to go away on a trip and rest get my mind together, and think what am I going to do next. I wish I had listened to my father about a lot of things. When do you want to leave? We can go out to the Lake do some fishing and we can sit around and talk. You need to talk to me because I know you got something on your mind. That sounds good. I need to go home and let father know I'm back. When I got home father said he was glad Cherry Etta didn't have to go to prison and how proud of me he was. Now son you done your job and you don't owe them anything. Forget about Cherry Etta and her family you know about them so stay away son. Promise me you will leave them along. Son your uncle needs your help in Mississippi he is back in trouble. What did Uncle Mark do now? I need you to go see your grandma she is very upset. When can you go son? As soon as I can I

need to get away it will do me good to go back home.
I'll leave tomorrow I need to call Dean and let him take
over some of my cases. I call Dean and told him I was
going to Mississippi and he said he was going too. He
wanted to spend some time with me. We caught the
plane the next day and flew to Mississippi I'm so glad I
have a friend like Dean but what is he going to say when
I tell him I have a black Mama. Father had called
Grandma Wilson and told her we were on our way.
Cousin William picks us up. at the Air Port. Grandma
was so glad to see us; Dean would come to Mississippi
with me doing the summer when school was out. She
was always nice to Dean. Anna Bell the maid was so
happy to see me she had cooked all the food that I like
and grandma call all the family to come over for dinner.
It was so nice to see everyone. After dinner grandpa ask
me to come out on the terrace with him. Henry your
father told me about you finding out about your Mama
and how you help her. How do you fell about that? Right
now grandpa I'm trying to think what I want to do. I
came here to help Uncle Mark and try to rest and try to
understand if I want her in my life. Father wants me to
stay away from them. What do you think grandpa? Son
you have to do what is in your heart you grown and you
have to make your own decisions. Whatever you decide
I love you and will be behind you all the way. You got
the Wilson blood running through your veins and I'm
proud of you son. Your father told me you his world he

wants me to talk to you and tell you to stay away from your Mama he thinks she will be nothing but trouble. He want you to one day be in the White House. I don't want to be in the White House someday. I want to be the lawyer I am. I'm happy for what I do. But I want you to think hard and good of what you may be getting yourself in to son. Thank, you grandpa. I think I'll listen to father. What about Uncle Mark what, did he do this time? He rob Sandy grocery store. There was a lot of witness. I don't understand why he keeps getting into trouble. We got money he doesn't have to keep getting into trouble. I think he sick Henry. I'll go tomorrow and see what I can do. We are well known family around here and got money you can almost get by with anything's here.

Grandpa owns his own cotton gin and he have a lot of people living on the plantation living here to pick cotton. He has a big garden for the women to work in. The women caned the food and Grandma take it to town and sale it. I went to town the next day to check on Uncle Mark and they said he wasn't getting out because he will be right back. He will have to wait until his court date. Dean and I went fishing, we went out and had fun, we met girls and party it sure took a lot off my mind while I was here. Dean didn't ask me what was on my mine. We went to court and prove Uncle Mark was a sick man and they let him go, and he had to get help. He was buck off a horse when he was young and hurt his head when he got older his head got worse. I got it to where he would spend the rest of his life in a nursing home. Grandpa didn't want him to spend it in prison. They will be able to go see him whenever they wanted to and he would be able to come home to visit, but he, would have to be supervise at all times when he was out of the nursing home. The night before Dean and I were to leave and come back home, my uncle Frank gave us a big going home party at his house he had so much food fish, shrimp, crawfish, corn, potato, lobster, and all the beer you could drink and so much more. Dean had a ball he was dancing, singing. We party all night long. The next morning we couldn't get out of bed so we had to stay one more day. My mind was so relax I forgot all about Cherry Etta and her kids. I made up my mind that I would stay away from her like my father, want me to. When, Dean and I was ready to leave Grandma Wilson ask me to stay away from them like my father wanted me too. She said Father had told her about me meeting Cherry Etta and the kids. She said father wanted her to talk me into staying in Mississippi and moving my law office there. I kiss grandma and told her I had to go back to my law office in the City. It's been three months and I haven't heard from Cherry Etta. Everything was going fine, I found me a girl friend and I was spending a lot of time with her. Dean told me he was ready to get married and start a family He fell in love. Dean (said) Henry I'm, glad you solve your problem you look so happy. I knew Dean wanted me to tell him what had been bothering me. I felt it wasn't the right time to tell him about my colored family. I don't want to lose his friendship. October 11, 1947 I heard a knock on my office door. Mr. Wilson Cora Jackson is here to see you she, don't have an appointment she said she will not leave until she talk to you if she had to stay all day and night. Oh shit what do she want now, send her in, hello Cora what are you doing here? Hi Henry It's about Cherry Etta. Who did she kill this time? I'm sorry Cora I can't help her any more I did my job I did what you ask me I will not help any more. I'm sorry. Cora my life is fine and my father will be mad at me if he, know I get mix up with you all again. I'm sorry Cora no, no. No. Henry Lee, will you be quite and let me talk, your Mama, have not kill nobody. She and the kids moved back here with me and I can't take, it she been here for two weeks and she back here on them, streets. When she lived in Derry she was real nice to people. She said she had to move back here because she couldn't live in that house any more because she had night mares about Tommy coming to get her. She though if she move back here he wouldn't be able to find her. What do you want me to do? I can't help her. She is a grown woman, she have to live her own life the way she want I'm sorry I can't help her. She is your daughter if she don't listen to you what make you think she will listen to me I don't even know her that well. Have she been here to see you since she been here? No and I don't want her too. I have done all I could for her. I just want to live my life like I have been. I don't want problems in my life I'm happy the way things are. I'm happy with the mother I have. I don't want to be a part of Cherry Etta life. What about your brother and sisters? They will be alright they use to the life they live. Cora she your child you deal with her. I know you don't mean what you saying, you are a good man. You don't want to forget us. All you have to do is tell her to find a job and take care of her kids, and stay off

Those streets it's not for her. There is nothing but trouble out there. She may listen to you. Cora I'll see what I can do. After Cora left I just sit there thinking if I should have listen to father to stay away from my mama. What can I do with a grown ass woman I don't ever, know. She is my mama and she should be telling me what to do. I said I would talk to her but not today I'm going home and enjoy the rest of my evening. On the way home a car came out of nowhere and hit me knock me into another car. I was thrown out of the car. I woke up two days later I open my eyes and the first thing I see is Cora and Cherry Etta. Henry, Henry Lee can you hear me. Baby this is your Mama Cherry Etta. I just laid there and said nothing. I was in no mood to talk to her or Cora. I didn't even know what was wrong with me. Cherry Etta (said) Henry you okay? Son you look so bad they said you have a broke, leg, and you have four broke ribs, and a lot of cuts and bruises.

But the doctor said you going live, you in a lot of pain. I still wouldn't say anything. She started to cry. Oh mama my baby can't talk. Cora came over to me and said Henry Lee you can't talk, I know you in a lot of pain. Then she started to pray for me. "God let this child live, he just found us and we would like to keep him in our lives a little longer heal his body let him get up and be able to walk out of this hospital, because his Mama need him in her life." Lord he just found us please let him stay here a little longer Lord if you do I will serve you for the rest of my life and do whatever you want me to do please Lord hear my prayer we need my grandson. Let your will be done Lord. I though, to myself oh God what in the world have I got myself into. I closed my eyes and though, they are my family. My side was in so much pain and I said oh my God. Cherry Etta started to cry again, Mama go get the doctor he, look like he is in so much pain. Next the nurse came in. Mr. Wilson you in pain, I gave you a pain shot 30 minute ago. I can't give you any more right now you have to give the one I gave you time to work. If you can go to sleep you will feel a little better. Would you like for me to tell everyone to leave? I could tell the nurse, wanted me to tell them to leave. Cherry Etta told the nurse you need to give him another pain shot now. I'm going to go find that doctor myself. Some damn body gone do something for my baby, look at him Mama, he look like he gone die. Cherry was still crying and she was getting on my nerves. You stay here Mama while I go find that doctor. I said no, no, no. Cora (said) oh you can talk I knew your ass was faking when your Mama was talking to you. Henry she is your Mama and she love you and she need to know if they gone help you. The nurse came back in the room. Mr. Wilson we can't discuss your record with anyone but your family, the lady that was in here said she was your mother and she have the right to do whatever she need to do for you. She said she, need to talk to your doctor right now, or somebody was going to get some ass kicking around here and she mean right now. She sure is a little woman to be talking like that. She, want to take you out of this hospital and put you in Saint Anthony hospital. Mr. Wilson should we put her out we know there is no way she could be your Mother. Before I could say anything Cora (said) she is his mama and we can do what the damn hell we please. I heard father (say) what the hell going on in here? He looked at Cora and (said) I said what the hell going on. The nurse (said) that lady said she is his mother and she was going to move him to another hospital. Father (said) this is his mother and I'm his father, and I want these damn people out of my son room right now I'm the one paying this damn hospital bill. I don't want them back in here do you understand me. I'm the one who say where he be moved to and I say what go, and nobody else. I don't want them back in this room do you hear me? Yes Mr. Wilson. Mom came over kiss me on the check and said baby everything will be all right. Father told Cora you get your ass out of here, you the one who started all this shit. I told you to stay away from my son and your damn daughter too. You stay away from him or I'll have your ass sent back to Mississippi. Cora (said) Robert you still a fool. When Cherry Etta walk back in the room, and saw father standing there her eyes got so big. Robert I'm having my son moved to another hospital. (He told her) I told you when my son was five years old to keep your ass away from him and I mean it now too. You lost your right when you gave him to me. And now you think you can bring your ass in here and try to tell people what to do about my son. You crazy as bitch get your ass out of here and take your Mama. If I see either of you back here I will make both your ass disappear. Cora and Cherry Etta ran out of the room and they never look back at me. My Mom was still holding my hand and Father look please. (Mom said) Henry I'll take care of you, you will be home before long. The nurse came back in the room and said who are those people, friends of yours. Father said they use to work for my family in Mississippi. This is his mother. Yes I can see he look just like her. Father told her he didn't want anyone in my room but family and my best friend Dean Carr and the people that work in my office. I don't want those two ladies back in here. Mr. Wilson can you tell me their names, so I can tell the night shift. Yes, Cora and Cherry Etta Jackson. I laid there and I could feel my body relax. It felt good having

Mom there with me. Mom is a very beautiful woman and she is very kind she always like helping others. She, take food to the homeless and do volunteer work. She always made sure I was happy. She never once told me that my Mama was a color woman. She never once made me feel uncomfortable. She always made me feel like I was her real son. She is real proud of me. Her friends think that I'm her real son. I believe Cora and Cherry Etta love me, but they make me feel like I owe them something. While I was in the hospital I had a lot of time to think what I had to do and I wanted my white family and friends. I love my Mom and father, and Barbara and Grandpa and Grandma Wilson, all my uncle and cousin in Mississippi. I don't ever want to give them up they have always been there for me. They are the only family I know. I want Dean in my life forever. So I made up my mind that I will stay away from my color family, they have too much drama in their lives. God why do people have kids that one day make them suffer for their mistakes? And put burdens on their kids, do they even care what happen to them. When they have sex I guess they only thinking of, themselves and don't give a damn about nothing else or who they hurt later in life. I'm going on with my life and put Cherry Etta out. But what about my brother and sisters, they had nothing to do with what my father and their mama did. I have Barbara and she is a wonderful sister, I know she don't know about me yet I don't know what she will say or do when she find out about me will it break her heart? How will father tell her he was once in love with a color woman and I'm, her half mix brother? I was in the hospital for four weeks. Dean wanted to pick me up. When I got home my Mom had a few friends over to welcome me home. Mom made a big fuss over me and Barbara surprise me and came home she was in Mississippi going to college. Mom and father were happy she was going to college in Mississippi. I got tired and Dean took me to my room. I'm glad I have Dean for a friend we have been through a lot doing the years. I sorry you in so much pain Henry I took over some of your cases for you. Thank you Dean. While I'm home I can work on some of them. After Dean left I relax and close my eyes I could see Cherry Etta crying. Lord she is my Mama. I can't let my father keep me away from her she need me. I won't tell my father when I see her. I was out of my office for four months and I haven't heard from Cora or Cherry Etta. So I just left things along I started to feel so good things was getting better my life was getting back together. Dean and some of my friends wanted to go on an Alaska cruise and wanted me to go with them, so I went with them it was the best time I had in a long time just being with my friends. I was gone for two weeks. When I got back home Mom wasn't feeling well and she didn't want to go to the doctor. The next morning I got up and went to the office. I was in my office about 30 mines Cherry Etta walk in. I was kind of glad to see her.

Hi Henry you feeling better. That damn daddy of, your is crazy. I didn't come back to the hospital to see you because I didn't want to upset you. And I didn't want to kick your daddy ass in that hospital. I call the hospital every day to check how you were doing I told them I was your Aunt Mary from Mississippi to see how you were doing and they would tell me. I was just so upset when I saw you. It's, okay I understand. How are Cora and the kids? That is why I'm here I need you to help me. It's Harold he went in to a store with some other kids and they stole some things and the owner press charges on him. He, have to go to court and I don't have any money. Will you be his lawyer? Where is Harold? He home they didn't take him to jail because he is too young. They told me I would have to bring him before a Judge. I'll see what I can do and I'll call you later. I call Cherry Etta a few days later and told her she didn't have to take Harold to court. I talk to the judge and Harold have, to go back to the store and tell the owner he sorry and he won't do it again, he have to give the owner 50 dollars, or work it out. Henry I ain't got that kind of money he will have to work it out it will teach him a lesson not to take thing that don't belong to him. Don't worry I'll take care of everything. Oh Henry I don't know what I'll do with, out you. I wanted to say to her what, did you do all the years I wasn't in your life.

You need to put Harold in something to keep him out of trouble. And you, need to stay out of the streets, it's not good for your kids to see you out there. Cora is too old you need to be taking care of her and the kids. What happen to you, when you were in Derry you had two jobs, and they said you were a good mother. Miss Ross really like you she has help you so much if it wasn't for her you maybe in prison right now and you pay her back by hanging out in the streets every day. Have you been back to Derry to see her? No I don't have a car, the one I had broken down and daddy sold it for junk, because I didn't have any money to pay him rent. Do you have a driving license? Yes. Well I'll see what I can do.

Oh thank you baby. I love you and you won't be sorry. I'll have a way to go find me a job. I could pay more attention to Harold if I had a place of my own. Mama house is to, small for us that is why we getting on her nerves if we could move off 2nd street I won't be down there and Harold won't be getting in to trouble all the time. Your sisters, is scare with all that go on down there. I'll see what I can do. She left my office just smiling. I though, of what my father said." Son you don't know what you getting into leave her along". I bought Cherry a 1947 Ford she was very happy. A month later, Cora, call me just crying. What is wrong now? What have Cherry and Harold done? It's not them it's your grandpa Thomas he is dead he had a heart attack what we gone do? I can't make it with, out Thomas. Cherry and the kids, is taking it very hard. She ran out saying she was thinking of Tommy being dead. These kids, is crying and I'm so nerves. Cora is Thomas still in the house? Yes the Funeral car just drove up. I'll be there in a few minutes. Damn, why do so much happen to these people. What the hell they did before they found, me. Why don't they leave me the hell along? I went to Cora house she and the kids, was still crying, the funeral car was just driving off when I got there. Shelly ran to me and said Henry I'm so happy to see you we don't know where Mama, she ran off down the street. Shelly she will be back. I told Harold to go down 2nd street to see if he saw his Mama. He came back and said he couldn't find her. Cora, ask me if I could go to the funeral home with her to take care of Thomas arraignments. Yes Cora I'll be back tomorrow, do you need anything else? No son I love you I don't know what I'll do without you. I ask Cora if Thomas had insurance. Yes we have a small one not much. Get it out and let me look at it for you. When she gave me the insurance paper it was only worth 200, hundred dollars. The next day I came back to pick Cora and Cherry Etta to go to the funeral home Cora said Cherry Etta never came home all night and she still wasn't home. We went to the funeral home and made the arraignments and I had to pay two hundred dollar more, three days later Thomas was buried. Cora and Thomas family was in Mississippi and none of them had money to come to Oklahoma. Cherry Etta and her kids were there and I was there and some of his friends. Cherry Etta said she was happy that I came and she thanks me for helping her mama. She never said where she was the pass few days. She started telling people that I was her son. They started to laugh at her. Girl Cherry Etta must be drunk saying that white boy is hers. After the funeral Cora ask me to go home with them for dinner. No Cora I need to go to work. I'll talk to you all later. I was so tired when I got to the office I pick up some papers and went home. I told father I just came back from Thomas funeral of course he was angry that I was still helping them.

Week later I got a call from congressman Evergreen to come to New York to take a case for him. He said his son was mix up in a murder. He said he heard that I never lost a case and I came highly recommended. I could name my price whatever I charge to save his son life. I told father that I was thinking about going to New York and take the case. Father ask me how long would I be. I don't know I believe it will take a long time maybe a year because he is a congressman son and I have to find out what happen and ask a lot of questions. Son please takes the case it will really help you in the long run, your name will be out there when you run for Senator, you need to get away for a while it will really do you good. I know the real reason he want me to take the case and that is to get away from Cherry Etta and Cora. I call Dean and told him I was going to New York and if he could take care of my cases and get someone to help him. Dean said he was going to and he will fly back and forth to take care of our big cases. I call the Congressman and told him I would be there in a few days and I was bringing my partner with me. When we got to New York we were pick up and drove to the Congressman home. He said he wanted us to stay with him in his home. He had a very big home like the one I lived in only a little bigger. There were six bedrooms' six bathrooms and a lot of servants to wait on us hand and foot it were real nice. Dean and I had our own room. Whatever we wanted was our, His son was there he was out on nine hundred thousand dollars bond. I ask him his name and he said Jeremy. How old are you Jeremy? I'm, 18 years old. Can you tell me what happen? (He said) I was at a friend house to a party with about twenty people. They were all drinking; my friend parents were out of town. A fight broke out and my friend Roger Taylor told everyone they had to leave. Everyone left and I pass out on the couch. When I woke up the next morning Roger was on the floor and we both had blood on our clothes. I didn't know what happen I didn't remember being is the fight. I ask Roger what in the world happen. He didn't remember either. There was trashed, beer cans, and liquor bottles everywhere, ashes was in the ash trays, the front door was open. Some of the tables were turn over, someone had got sick and it was all in a corner. My head was hurting so bad I laid back down. I don't know how long I was sleep when I heard Mr. and Mrs. Taylor yelling at Roger. "What in the hell went on here; get your ass up right now before I kill you". Mrs. Taylor told me to get up and go home she was calling my mother. When I got up to leave I heard Mrs. Taylor screaming we ran to see what she was screaming about. We got to the bed room and blood was everywhere and our friend Janice Baker was laying on the floor covered in blood. Mr. and Mrs. Taylor looked at us and saw blood on us, he said what is the hell have you boys done, who in the hell is this girl? Mr Taylor calls the police. When the police came they ask us what happen. We didn't know because we had passed out. We tried to tell them we didn't do it they didn't believe us because we had blood on us. Police read us our rights and took us to jail. We stay in jail a week my father and Roger father paid bail. It was all over the news that Roger and I had something to do with Janice murder and they wanted to know what happen. I didn't know what happen, I feel so bad that I couldn't remember what happen. I do know Roger and I had nothing to do with her murder. Jeremy, can you remember any of the people that were there? Yes. I need you to write the names down for me. Mr Wilson do you think you can help me? I don't believe I could do anything like that Janice was my friend I like her. I'll do my best son you get me those names as soon as you can. I have a lot of work to do and I need a lot of answers.

Congressman Evergreen (said). Henry will you please help my son I can't believe he would do anything like this he and Roger are good boys, in my heart they couldn't do anything like this. Congressman I will have to have Dean to help me. Don't, worry I'll pay the two of you to do whatever it take to help my son. I don't know my way around New York I'll need detectives also. I don't care what you need just save my son; I have a bright future for him. Dean and I started questing some of the people who were at the party. We went to the police station to get all the information we could. I talk to the D A to see what charge was being charge on Jeremy. The DA name was Bruce Porter, I was told he was a hard man and didn't like to lose he want to charge the two boys with rape and first degree murder. I'm a good man and I don't like to lose either. I know I have to really work hard on this case, after I talk to the boys I felt they were telling me the truth but I have to prove it. I found out Janice Baker was rape and murder and was stab fifteen times. I told Dean we would have to move out of the Congressman house and move to a hotel because I didn't want to see their faces every day asking me so many question about the case, we would have to go in and out of their house a lot. Looking at their faces every day and trying to work on the case would be too much for me I need to be able to think and get a lot of answer to win my case. I knew it would be hard to prove his son case because he and Roger were the only ones left in the house and they both had blood on them. I knew if Dean and I solve this we would get big name cases I knew we would be all over the news if we solve this case and we could name our price.

One day I was going in the Hotel one reporter walk up to me and ask me to tell him about myself and why did I take this case of two guilty men. I kept on walking I wasn't ready to answer any news reporter. He kept asking me Mr Wilson tell, us who you really are. Where did you get your law degree? Are you the son of Oil Million Airs Robert Wilson? Why you taking this case? Are you friends with Congressman Evergreen?

Do you think you can win this case? I kept on walking. ? Do you believe they are guilty? The reporter (said) Mr. Wilson do you think you can find them not guilty like you did Cherry Etta Jackson? When he said that my heart stop beating, Dean looks at me and said, that is the lady you found not guilty in Derry Oklahoma, Mr. Wilson, Mr. Wilson! I kept walking to the Hotel. Dean wanted to know why I was so quite. Henry Lee what's wrong did that reporter say something to you that you didn't like? Should I tell Dean now that Cherry Etta is my mama? I wasn't ready to tell him. I didn't know what he would think of me having a black Mama, Dean could always tell when I had things on my mind. I can't talk about Cherry Etta right now I have to keep my mind on this case. I told him I had my mind on the case because this will be the biggest case I had. The next morning I told Dean I wanted to find some more people I could talk to that was at that party. We found a young man name Chuck Thompson. He said when he was leaving he saw Janice going up stair. Jeremy had pass out on the couch. He thought everything was all right because everyone was leaving. I didn't know anything had happen. Janice drove her own car so I knew she was okay she wasn't drunk. Do you know what the fight started about?

Yes it was some guys I didn't know, they just came in; they said they saw a party and they just wanted to know if someone was there they knew. We were all drinking so no one said anything to them. The guys started messing with some of the girls there and they didn't want them touching them because they were pretty wasted. Roger told them to get out and one of the guys started to fight Roger. Roger told everyone to leave. The guys left. My friend Frank and I was leaving I told Roger I would see him later he sit down in a chair and That's all I know. How many guys were there? It was three of them. Frank and I left. Thank you Chuck if you remember anything else please contacts me. Chuck can you remember what time it was when you left. It was 3:30 am Sunday morning. Thank you if you remember anything else call me here is my card I'm at the Hill Top Hotel. Dean and I went back to the hotel, when we got in the room Dean said Henry you did it again. Did what? You had that look on your face when that reporter asks you who Cherry Etta Jackson was. Why would he ask you about her? Don't lie to me Henry what' going on with you? Henry we been friends a long time and you know I love you like a brother we always tell each other everything so talk to me man. Dean I wanted to tell you when I first found out about Cherry Etta Jackson but I don't know what you would think of me, when I tell you what I found out. I didn't think you will be my friend again. What is it Henry? There is nothing you can say will stop me for caring about you or loving you. When the reporter said her name you really look scare. Why was the reporter asking you about her? Because she is my mother and I have two sisters and a brother by her. I just found out before I took her case. Dean looked at me and (said) man you lying to me, she's a color woman. You're white, stop playing with me Robert and Becky is your parents. There is no way that woman could be your mother. If you don't want to tell me what's wrong with you, okay you don't have to make up a lie. Dean I'm not lying to you. Her mother came is my office and told me to save her daughter that is when she told me who her daughter was. I went to her house and I saw a picture of father with this black woman and he was holding me in his arm. I couldn't believe it I didn't know what in the world was going on. I went home and told Father I went to Cora house and Cora told me about him and Cherry Etta. He confess everything to me he didn't want me to know my mother was black. I wanted to meet her and see what she was like that is one of the reasons I took her case. You remember when we went on 2nd street when we were 16 and saw the man shoot that man, he died and the man that shot him was the father of my brother and sisters. I be damn Henry, are you telling me the truth there is no way in hell that woman could be your mother you look white I never had any idea. I be damn you a color boy. I need me a drink. I looked at Dean and I knew he would have nothing, else to do with me. After he had a drink he looked at me and said Henry Lee Wilson I don't give a damn what color you are, blue, black. Red, or green, you my best friend and I want you in my life forever I love you man. We can work through this. Dean hugs me and I broke down and cried. Dean every time they need anything I been helping them because I feel sorry for them. Father is mad at me for being around them every time Cora call, he don't want his friends to know that he has a son by a black woman. I just came out white that is the reason he wanted me. Dean I'm not ready to tell anyone else right now because I need to get myself together and learn how to deal with this myself. Dean don't tell your father right now because you know how he feel about color people I know when he find out I will no longer be welcome in your home. Yes Henry it's our secret, man Henry why did your father not tell you did he think you would never find out? He said that he would tell me one day when he thought the time was right. My father love color people he always helping them but he just wanted me to have everything that money could buy and not having kids tease me anymore. I got your back Henry I'll all ways be your friend. Dean that mean, a lot to me thank, you. I'm going to stay here in New York until after the case is close I don't want to be under a lot of stress I know if I go back home Cora and Cherry Etta will need something. I know it may come out in the news. Reporter may already know. I hope it don't hurt my father and mother when their friends find out. I know my father will say "I told you to stay away from them now they will ruin your life". Dean you have to take care of your cases and help me with mines back home. Okay you right I got to get back I have a case Friday. I'll try to help you all I can Henry. Dean you are a real good friend thank you. Dean left the next morning going back to Oklahoma City. I call father and told him that I told Dean about me and Cherry Etta and what the news reporter said.

Father I'm sorry for not listening to you I shouldn't have taken this case in New York the reporters will find out all they can about me. I tried to tell you to listen to me and this time son listen to what I going to tell you, I don't want you to be unhappy I love you and I want you to stand up and be the man you are and take whatever come your way I'm here for you and I will stand beside you till the end, you need me to come to New York to help you I'm on my way. Sometime son God play tricks on us you don't have to pay for the mistakes I made it's time I stand up for my own damn life and the choice I made. I have kept Cherry Etta a secret all these years

Your grandfather always told me to tell you when you were younger he said secrets always find a way to come out I don't know what will happen I will be there for you whatever you decide to do. Thank you father tell mother I love her, I'll call you in a few days. After I hung up with father I sit there thinking what I am going to do I knew I had to keep my mind on this case and not worry about Cherry Etta and Cora. I had to find out if Roger and Jeremy killed Janice; I want to work hard to find out what happen. I wanted to get this case solved before I went to court because I don't like to lose a month has gone by and I wanted to go home for a few days. When I got home Barbara was home. Boy I was so happy to see her, she is a beautiful young lady Father and mother though it was time to tell Barbara about me before she find out from someone else. After dinner father (said) Barbara I need to tell you something. When I was a young man in Mississippi I fell in love with a young black girl her name is Cherry Etta Jackson I had a very handsome son by her and I love him with all my heart and there is nothing in this world I wouldn't do for him. Where is he do you get to see him? Why are you just telling me? Henry do you know him have you seen him? "Yes I have". Do mother know about him? Yes baby I know him and I love him so much. He means the world to me. Why haven't anyone told me about him" Because Baby I didn't tell him and I didn't want any of my friends to know. I'm telling you because Henry Lee is working on that case in New York and it may come out, a report want to know about his mother. Where is he? I'm here. You here what you talking about Henry? You guys tell me everything now. Cherry Etta Jackson Is my mother I just found out a few months ago. Mother what are they talking about? Baby I'm not Henry real mother. You guys playing with me Henry is white like me. How can his mother be black? Barbara its true baby, Henry real mother is Black … Why are you just telling me? I plan to tell you and Henry one day when I felt the time was right. I'm sorry. Henry you didn't know. No I just found out a few months ago. Barbra looked at me and walks over and hugs me. Henry I love you I know you were hurt when you found out. Are you okay now? No I'm still in shock. Have you met your Mother? Yes. Do you want her is your life? Yes only because I have a brother and two sisters I feel sorry for them. Why? Because they need help and their mother needs help with them, they are nice kids. Will you take me to meet them? I looked at father and he didn't say a word. Deep down in my father heart I felt he didn't want Barbara near Cherry Etta and her kids. Someday Barbara but not right now I would like everything a secret for now. None of my friends know but Dean. What did he say? He said he didn't care who I was he loved me and we will always be best friends. I love you to Henry and you will always be my brother, and who ever have anything to say about it can go straight to hell. Father was happy for what

Barbara said, and how she took the news. I didn't call Cherry Etta or Cora while I was home I stayed a week. I left and went back to New York, a few days later Dean, call and said Cora keep calling for me and he didn't know what she wanted and he didn't tell her where I was. He asks her what she wanted with me but she wouldn't tell him, he said he told her he would help her because I was out of town and would be gone for a while. Dean find out what she want and let me know. The next day Dean calls and said she told him Harold was in trouble again for beating a kid at school and he was suspended for three days, and she needed me to get him help get back in school. Dean told her he would take care of everything. Cherry Etta was getting in trouble also he had to get her out for jumping on a lady on second street Cherry beat the lady so bad the lady had to go to the hospital. Just because the lady told her she didn't know why her mama name, her Cherry because she was too black to be a cherry. Cherry was charged with assault and brattier. Dean said he went to the school talk to the principal and they Harold come back in two days. I told Dean I would pay him because I knew they didn't have money to pay him; Dean took care of everything for me. I couldn't worry about them right now I had to keep my mind was on my case. I stayed away as long as I could so they started to call Dean every time they need anything. January 1948 Jeremy and Roger trial started, I proved they were not guilty they had nothing to do with

Janice murder. One of the young men Roger put out of the house confess because he couldn't live with himself knowing what he did to her. He kept seeing her over and over in his mind and what he did to her. He said they came back to the house the lights were still on and the door was open and Janice was leaving and they made her go back in the house they wanted to party with her. She tried to leave and one of the boys hit her. Roger and Jeremy was pass out we took Janice up stair one of the boys push her on the bed and we rape her she said she was going to call the police and we took turn stabbing her. We knew she was dead so we took the knife and wipe blood on Jeremy and Roger so they could be charge with her murder we wanted to get even with Roger for putting us out. The young man cried and cried and told Roger and Jeremy he was so sorry the other guys made him help them. They put the blood on their shirts so no one would look for them. I'm so sorry I was drinking and we just wanted to have fun. He said he couldn't sleep at night so he had to tell the truth. I found all three boys guilty of her murder and was sent to prison for life. After the trial was over I was ready to get home to Oklahoma. Congressman Evergreen and Senator Taylor paid me twenty thousand dollars each, because the trial lasted for two months. That was a lot of money for two months work. I left two days later, for home. It has been over a year since I met Cherry Etta and Cora, but it's seemed like years. When I got back I went home. I didn't go to my office for a few days.

I wanted to rest for a while. Father and I went out to our summer home on the lake for the weekend. We took the boat out and fished. It felt good to be out there just the two us. We did a lot of talking. Father still thinks I should leave Cora and her family alone. I told father that I like New York and one day I may move there. He was all for it, because I wouldn't be around Cora and Cherry Etta. I really like New York. I would have to try to find me a law office there, and see if I could talk Dean into finding him a new partner to run our law office. After, father, and I come home Sunday evening, Mom had Dean and his family was over for dinner. We talked about my trip to New York, father told them I may move there and he was hoping I would run for Senator one day. Dean said if you go I may want to go also because there is good money to make there. Monday morning I got up and went to the office, I had just sit down to read some case papers when my secretory came in. Mr. Wilson, Cora Jackson is here to see you. Tell her that I'm not here. Henry Lee why you lying to me? Cora was standing by the door. If you don't want to be bothered with me just say so, you don't have to lie. I been calling you for two months and you never call me back that white boy you sent to help me don't know nothing.

Yes, he help Harold get back in school, but he can't do anything with Cherry Etta.

Henry Lee I'm tired. I can't take it no more! I want her and them damn kids out of my house and I want to be left the hell alone! Since Cherry Etta came back here after killing Tommy, she thinks she is tuff acting like she ain't scared of nobody. I think she carry a gun because she feels you going to get her out of anything she does. She needs to keep her ass off 2nd street because it's too much going on there. Cora started to cry. Henry Lee I want you to send me back to Mississippi so I can get away from them damn fools. Okay Cora, I'll talk to her.

The next day I went to Cora house to see if I could talk to Cherry. When I got there, Cora said Cherry had found her a boyfriend and she didn't come home last night. Cora said she don't know where she was. I saw Shelly and Carrie; they had grown a lot. They were very pretty girls. Shelly smiles a lot, and said she was going to Douglas High school and was on the honor roll. She said she wanted to one day be a lawyer. Carrie was in Dunbar school and she was making good grades too. Harold also went to Dunbar school, his grades were bad, and he was getting in trouble a lot.

I ask where was Harold and they said he was somewhere down the street. I told Cora I would be back later I had to be in court all day. I got so busy I had to be in court for a week. When I went back to Cora house to see Cherry, Harold came to the door, what you want he said. Who call you to come here? You come to tell us our mama is back in jail? No, I came to see Cora is she here? Cora was in bed. I felt sorry for Cora, and I began to like her. She was getting so old fast. Cora is you all right? She looks so bad and so sick. Cora said she was 69 years old and she sure looks older since I saw her just last week.

Cora what's wrong let me take you to a doctor. Where is Cherry Etta? I don't know she hasn't been here in a week she haven't called and checks on her kid's. I don't know if she dead or not. I sent Harold down there on the streets to find her and he couldn't. They said they saw her with her new boyfriend and nobody knows where they were. How long you been sick? Only a few days Shelly, been taking care of me." You should have called me. Do you want me to call the Ambulance? No, I ain't dead yet. Shelly help, Cora get dressed. I'm taking her to the hospital. The kid's said they didn't want to be left alone and that they were going too.

I took Cora to University Hospital. They said they were keeping her for a few days to run tests. I took the kid's back home and Cherry still wasn't home. I told the kid's they would have to go with me. I couldn't leave them there alone. I told them to pack their clothes and bring whatever they wanted. Shelly said they couldn't because if they leave everything that they had; it would be gone when they came back. If they do Shelly we will get more things. Where are you taking us? You're going to my house until Cora comes home.

I didn't know what my father was going to say when I bring them home. I knew I couldn't leave them there. When I drove up in the yard, Harold said, "Wow! Wow! Do you live here? This is the biggest house I ever saw. Are we going to live here with you? Yes until Cora or Cherry Etta come for you. When I came in, mom and father were in the sun room. I told our maid Donna, to take them to the kitchen and give them something to eat. I went in. Mom and father was sitting at the table having a snack, because it was beautiful, Mom love flowers and it look like it was outside Hi Mom, father. Hi son what you doing home so early? Is anything, wrong? Father I bought some one home with me, to stay for a few days. Oh, who is it? Father please don't get upset.

I all most knew my father thought it was Cora or Cherry Etta. I could see the mad look in his eyes. Just as I was going to tell them Barbara came out and said Henry Lee those kid's sure are nice looking! That little Carrie is so cute! What damn kid's (My father said)! My Mom said "what are you talking about Barbara? Henry Lee, brother and sisters. Henry Lee I know you didn't bring those damn kid's in my house without asking me? Did you bring their damn mama to? Please Father, calm down. Let me explain. Cherry Etta is gone somewhere and they don't know where she is. I had to take Cora to the hospital. They said she had to stay a few days. I don't know what is wrong with her and I couldn't leave the kid's by themselves.

Robert, just calm down we will work out something. Where are the kid's (mom said)? Barbara (said) they in the kitchen. My mom and Barbara got up and went in the kitchen. Barbara acts like she was happy to have them in the house. Mom was happy also. Father, well he wanted me to be happy and I know he wants them out of his house as soon as they could go. Barbara said she would take care of them until I go to the hospital to check on Cora. When I got there Cora was so unhappy. The doctor said she was really run down. She didn't have any vitamins in her body. She had a very bad kidney infection. She said she hasn't been eating. She was worried about her daughter, she hasn't heard from her. Cora's blood pressure was high. They said she had to stay in the hospital, until they could get her pressure down and some of the infection from her kidneys. I stayed with Cora for a while and told her I would be back the next day. I gave the hospital my phone number to call and I told them I would take care of her hospital bills. I wanted her to have the best of care. When I got back home to check on the kid's, Barbara, and Shelly liked each other. My mom and Barbara took the girls shopping. Harold stayed with my father. Harold ask father so many questions. He told him he didn't have a father his mama killed his dad and he started to cry. My father talked to Harold and found out why Harold was always in trouble. He found out why he was mad at his mama. He told my father he didn't want to listen to his mama because she was not a good mama. Harold believed he didn't have to listen to her. He said he wish his mama was dead too and he didn't care if she came back for him. He said she could stay where ever she was.

My father looked at him and said "son come here." Father put his arms around Harold, and said son it will be all right. I was so shocked. Father put his arms around my brother; He told Harold that things will be different from now on. He even told Harold he could go upstairs. I looked at my father, and couldn't believe what he had said to Harold. Henry Lee, what do you want to do about these kids? I don't know. I'll talk to Cora to find out what she want to do. The kids can stay here until Cora Come home from the hospital. Cora was in the hospital a week. My mom told me to bring Cora to the house so she could be with the kids. Cora was so happy that we took care of the kids and would let her stay also.

When I bought Cora to the house, she couldn't believe I live in such a beautiful home. She loved it. She loved being waited on by our servants. She said "Robert thank you for letting us live here with you and your family. Father looked at her and said "Huh" and walked out of the room. Robert is still the same. He will be okay Cora. Things were going well. Father had our driver to take the kids to school every day and pick them up. Harold was happy and back in school, and doing very well. Harold and my father was getting along real good. The girls miss their mama but Harold, didn't care. He loved living in our big house.

Cora and my mom were happy. Cora was teaching mom how to make quilts. They would talk a lot. I was happy that I could come home every day and relax. Things were going good. My father liked Harold and the girls. I came home one evening and Harold and father were in the back yard. He was teaching Harold to play golf. Dean came over and couldn't believe father had changed. I was so happy Dean was still in my life. He liked the kid's also. Two months have gone by and we still haven't heard from Cherry Etta. Cora was so worried about her.

Henry Lee, can you find my baby? The only time she been away from me was when she was in Derry, and I knew where she was. Something is wrong. She would never leave her kids this long." Cora started to cry. "Henry Lee, we need to keep calling the police to see if they come up with anything yet. I had filed a missing report on Cherry Etta a week after she didn't come home. "Henry Lee, your mama was always out there on them street. I hope she ain't dead. I heard she met a man name Wayne Moore. She been letting him drive her car you bought her. Maybe they gone out of town and she can't call home. They said he was a drug addict. He may have her on drugs too. I just don't know where she is. Cora I '11 do all I can to find her. Don't worry.

Henry Lee I love living here and I thank Robert for letting me and the kid's live here, but it's time we went home. Cora you need to stay here so someone can take care of you. You can't live back in that house. Why do you want to leave here? That's been my home ever since I been here. Thomas worked hard to buy that house. I just miss my own home. When Cherry come back she won't know where to find me and the kids. Shelly and Carrie were born in that house. I miss my friends on 2nd street. Cora the kid's don't need to go back down there, just stay a little while longer and I will see what I can do. I went to my mom and father to see what I could do to help them. Father said he understood that Cora wanted to be around her own people. She doesn't want to be around white folks. You and your mom go down there and see if you can find a better house for them.

A few days later mom and I found a house on 8th street. It was a real nice house; it had three bedrooms, bath and a half, and another room that was used as an office. A doctor lived there; he moved out of state and had the house up for sale. I bought the house for them. The kid's would have their own bed room. My mom said Harold could use the office for his bedroom. My mom help fix the house up. We bought new furniture for the house and we moved some of Cora and the kid's things in the house. Cora I need you to come and go with me.

Are you feeling okay? I'm fine where you taking me? Just follow me. My Mom, father, and Cora got in the car with me and we drove to the house on 8th street.

Cora said why you taking me to Doctor Johnson house? Why you taking me to see him are something wrong with me? Henry Lee, I going to die? No Cora this is your new home. What? What you say? Oh my God! Stop playing with me Henry. Henry I can't live here! Why Cora? Cause I, am not rich like Doctor Johnson. I got no money to pay for this house and I don't have enough money to pay the rent on a house like this. I'm too old to try to pay for a house like this. Cora I bought this house for you and the kids to live here. Oh my God what you do that for? I don't know what I'm going to do with you, Cora. Come on let's go in to see if you like the house.

We went in the house and Cora just started crying and crying Oh my God! This is nice. I ain't, never had nothing in my life this nice. Don't worry Cora; I will help you take care of the house. Cora stood there and she got real quiet and kept standing there not moving. My father said Cora you alright? I'm so worried about Cherry Etta, where is she? I haven't heard anything. Lord where is my baby? Cora we have someone looking for her. My friend Dean is helping us too. We will find her.

We left Cora at her new home and we went back to get the kids to bring them to their new home. The girls were happy to be back on the east side. They wanted to be with their friends. Shelly said she could walk to school and maybe the kid's would stop teasing her bout having a driver to drive her to school. Carrie was happy because she could ride the bus. Harold said he like our house and he didn't want to leave he was happy there. He hasn't been in any kind of trouble since he live with us. Harold told my father he loved him and he didn't have a dad. My father had fallen in love with Harold, they would go fishing together, they would take long walks together and they had long talks together. My father didn't want him to go either. Mom ask our maid Donna if she would move in with Cora and the girls to help them and she would give her a nice raise

Father and mom took Harold on our boat for a few days because he didn't want to go back to live with Cora. Harold loved the water. He was doing very well with my father and I was happy that he loved my brother too. Our driver was still taking Harold to school. He said he didn't care about the kid's teasing him about having a white family. He was doing well in school and still staying out of trouble. My father would help him with his homework and would make him read books. Father said he was training him to be a doctor or lawyer.

Harold liked having my father around. He had started to call him Pop's. We were having dinner one night and I ask father to pass me the rolls and Harold said Henry Lee why do you call Pop's father, that is what old men call their Dad and you are not old. My father laughed, and laughed and said yes Henry Lee, you too young to call me father. Mom laughed also, Barbara said she was tired of calling him father too. So Barbara and I said we would call him Dad.

It has been one year now and we still haven't heard from Cherry Etta, I wondered why did she leave without telling me or Cora or even telling her kids goodbye. I wonder if the man she was with had did something to her. She had been hanging out on the streets, and running with bad folks. My Mom would go over to check on Cora and the girls. She made sure they were taken care of. It was a lot of pressure off me. I could do my work so much better. After winning the case in New York I been getting so many high power cases that I had to turn some of them down. Dean said I had been working so hard and had so much on my mind, I needed a break and he had a big party for me at his house. While I was there I ran into an old girlfriend of mines, Katie Martin. We had a nice time and decided to see each other again.

I started to spend a lot of time with her. I invited her to my house one night for dinner. When she came we all sit and ate our dinner together in the dining room. Harold was sitting at the table, and she said "whose cute young man is this? What is your name? Harold." Nice you meet you Harold, my name is Katie. (Harold smiled). Whose son, Donna's? No Katie. After dinner we will talk. Come and sit beside me. Mom and Dad were so happy to see her. They ask her about her family and we did a lot of small talk. I ask Katie if she would like to go in my room because we need to talk. Katie, after I tell you something you may never want to see me again. I don't know how you will feel about me, after I tell you somethings about me you don't know. What Henry? You got me curious.

Katie come and sits beside of me. Harold is my brother and I have two sisters beside Barbara.

Your brother, what do you mean? You never told me this. I found out two years ago. I told Katie everything and about Cherry Etta, and Cora. She looked shocked like she couldn't believe I had a black Mama. She always thought Becky was my Mom. She said my dad didn't look like the type of man that loved black women. "Wow, Henry Lee this is a shock. I told you that you wouldn't want to see me after what I told you. I'm half black. Henry Lee I'm so shock for what you just told me, will you take me home?

When we got there she asks me to please come in for a few minutes. Would you like to have a drink? Yes, I would. Well what do you think of my family? I haven't met your family, if they are all like Harold, I think I would. Are you sure Katie? I love you Henry! I always have. I left Oklahoma City because your Dad had plans for you to go to college and at that time I didn't fit in. You were so busy going to law school I didn't want to stand in your way. I'm back now and I will never leave you again. I love you too much. I don't care what you are or who you are, all I know is I love you Henry Lee Wilson. I grab her, I kiss her and I took her in my arms. I kept kissing her and we made love. I spent the night with her. The next day I was so happy.

Four weeks later I ask Katie to marry me. Four months later, we were married and Dean was my best man. We had a big wedding it was over a hundred people there. Cora and the girls were there, and so was Harold. By then my Dad loved Harold like his own son. Mom and Barbara loved them too. We still haven't heard from Cherry Etta, when I go to see Cora she would say Henry Lee my baby is dead, she wouldn't never leave these kid's with me this long, without coming back to see them. We had no idea where to find her. Six more months have gone by and still no Cherry Etta.

One day I got a call from Ethel Ross, in Derry. She wanted to know if I could come see her. I went to Derry to see Ethel and (she said.) Henry Lee, I'm getting old, and I have nobody. Joe, he gave me some money to take care of me for a long time, because he knew his folks wouldn't give me anything when he died. I want to leave my money and my home to Cherry Etta and the kids. I been trying to get in touch with her and she must have moved because my letter came back. I want you to draw up my will. This here house is for all of them but I want my money split with each of them. I want each one of them to get the same amount and I want you to take care of the kid's money until they get old enough to take care of their own money.

I want you to take out what I need to pay you for helping me. Ethel are you alright? Are you planning to die? Sometime we all gone die. We don't want to but there's nothing we can do about it, when God get ready for us we got to go. You're right Ethel. I'll get everything ready for you and I will come back and read it to you. And you can sign it. How is' Cherry Etta and the kids? I don't know I haven't heard or seen her in over a year. Well she came through with her boyfriend and I told her he was no good. Just like that old Tommy; he was bout like him. I told her to leave him alone, bcause she gone end up killing him. They stayed all day with me; she said she was on her way to Nebraska. And she would stop by on her way back to Oklahoma City. She ask me for some money to help her out and I gave her a hundred dollars."

She said she would be back to see me. I didn't like that ass hole she was with I told her to be careful and she told me, Ethel you know I ain't scared of nobody now. I'll kill his ass if he messes with me. I got a gun in my purse. I told her my prayers was with her and she better not use that gun on nobody because you may not be able to help her next time and she just laughed at me. She (said) oh my Henry Lee can get me out of anything. So they left and I ain't seen or heard from her since. I thought she was busy taking care of her mama and those kids. If I hear from her Henry I'll call you. Thank you

Ethel, I promise you I'll be back. I hug her and when I drove off she was still setting under that tree.

I came back to Oklahoma City and made out her will. A week later I came back to Derry to bring Katie, Shelly, Carrie and Harold wanted to come with me to see Ethel. When we got to Ethel's house she wasn't sitting under the tree. I got out, went to the door knocked. Ethel (said) come on in. When I came in she was sitting in a chair. Hello Ethel, I was worried you weren't under the tree. Well son I have to come in the house s o m e t i m e. You said you would be back. Yes and I bought someone to see you. I'll be back. I went to the car and told everyone to get out. The kids got out and ran inside to see Ethel. They were so happy to see her and she was happy to see them. Hello Miss Ross. Oh my goodness, you kids sure have grown. You sure are, good looking kids. I'm so glad to see you.

They all hug Ethel. When I bought Katie in, she (said) "now who is this pretty young thing?" This is my wife, Katie. "Your wife Well I be damn you done got married." Yes. Well how you Miss Katie Henry Lee told me so much about you Miss Ross I wanted to come and meet you too. Well let me get up and cook you folks some food. I know you going to stay until I cook. Well Ethel, we have to get back to the City. "Sit your ass down Henry Lee, these kid's got to eat. I know they are hungry. Shelly come on in here and help me. Ethel,

Katie and I are going to town do you need anything? No. When you get back the food will be ready.

When we got to town we went to the courthouse. I wanted to see if Judge Reid was still there. When we walked into his office I ask Joyce if Judge Reid was still there. "Yes he is. Oh I remember you. You're Cherry Etta Jacksons' lawyer. How is she doing? I don't know I haven't seen her lately. Let me see if the Judge will see you. He said come on in. Well hello there young man, who is the pretty lady you got there with you? This is my wife Katie. "Hello Judge, Henry Lee told me about you and I wanted to meet you. Sure hope it wasn't all too bad. No he really likes you. What, you doing in Derry now son? I came to see Ethel.

What the hell she done? Nothing Judge I came to help her with some business. What kind of business? I all ways take care of Ethel. Why she didn't come to me? I'm just getting her affairs in order. "What she going to die?" No judge not that I know of. Would you and your wife like to have a drink? No Judge we just wanted to come by and see you. I thought you and Ethel would be married by now, what happen? I ask her and she turn me down. She said, Joe you old fool we to old now, just leave things like it is. But I still love her and there is nothing in this world I wouldn't do for her, we still friends. She come to my house some times and helps me out. I know she still love me too. It's nice seeing you Judge we have to leave. Good to see you to son, you and your lovely wife come back and see me some times. We will.

Katie liked the way all the stores were around the court house in a square. We walked around to some of the stores, and we sure liked the nice people we met in Derry. We went back to Ethel house to pick up the kids so we could leave. Ethel had cooked a nice dinner for us Katie really like the food. She ate like she hadn't eaten in days. She told Ethel she was coming back to get some more of her good cooking. It made Ethel happy to have us there and the kid's. I gave Ethel her Will and ask her to read it to make sure she was happy with what I did.

She left the kid's one thousand dollars each, and Cherry Etta one thousand. Her home was for all of them and her land she had next door; if one of them wanted to come back to Derry and build them a home on it. If the house was sold she wanted the money to be split equally with the four of them or they could buy out each other. She had one thousand left and wanted me to give her a real good funeral, at Mt Olive Church on Grove Street. All the money left over she want me to keep it for my bill she owe me. She signs the papers and asks me to keep them in a safe place.

She wanted me to always take care of Cherry Etta and the kid's because they was like a family to her and she felt sorry for them. Ethel I'm sorry but we have to leave. I'm sorry you all have to leave but if you hear from Cherry Etta call me. I will Ethel. We all hug her and said goodbye. As I was walking out of the door she said, Henry Lee, here take this letter and put it with my stuff and open it after my death. Bring the kid's back to see me sometimes. I will. When we drop the girls off Katie and I went in to see Cora. Katie likes Cora too. Harold said he was going back home with me. Cora was still sad she still hasn't heard one thing from her daughter. I was wondering about Cherry. I couldn't understand how she could leave her mama and kid's and never call them.

The next day when I went into the office I told Dean what Ethel said about Cherry going to Nebraska? Dean said he would work on it for me. He had her picture put in the paper and filed a missing report with the police department in Nebraska. A year and six months have pass and I figure she was dead or didn't want any of us to know where she was. I figured she may be on drugs so bad she couldn't remember where she came from. I still haven't heard from my mama Cherry Etta. I decide to go on with my life and take care of Cora. The kid's went on with their lives and we were happy. Cora, she was getting old and she looked so tired and unhappy all the time. I did all I could to find her daughter and I couldn't. There was nothing else I could do.

March 15, 1949, Judge Reid called me and said E t h el had died. I told him I would come and help him make her funeral arrangements. It was what she wanted. Katie and I went to Derry and Judge Reid looked so old from the last time I saw him. He told me now his whole world was gone and he had nothing to live for. The two women he loved have left him alone (he said). You know Henry, I miss Ethel so much. She was the only woman that could make me happy and she always made me laugh. She was always cussing me out about my drinking. But she understood why. She knew I never got over my son death because I didn't know if he suffered before he died. I always wonder where that bastard had my son before he was found. I know he killed him. I'm so sorry Judge. What can I say or do to help you? I know how much Ethel loved you. She told me the last time I talk to her she ask me to see about you and help you after she was gone. She worried about you Judge. "Yes I know."

Judge do you want to go to the funeral home with me? No son you take care of everything for me. I know you will do the right thing. Ethel belongs to Mt Olive Church. Two days later Katie and the kids came back with me to her funeral Judge Reid cried the whole time. The kid's took it hard also. They loved Ethel. They said she was like a grandma. She was buried at Grace Hill Cemetery. I asked Judge Reid to come back to Oklahoma City with us for a while or just for a few days. I thought it would help him to be around some one. Katie talked him in to going back with us.

Dad and Mom were happy to have him there and he was happy to get out of Derry for a few days. Dad took him to play golf and they went fishing. After a few days, he said he needed to go back home and check on things. Dad told him he was welcome to come back any time. While we were on our way back, to Derry Judge Reid said Henry why didn't you tell me Cherry Etta was your mother? Are you shame of her? Yes sometimes. Your Dad, told me about things when we went fishing. Look like our family has something in common. Your Dad told me how Cherry had changed after she came back to the City. You know son we can't pick our folks, no matter who they are or what they are. We just have to forgive them and put them in God hands.

When I first met you I had a feeling about you. I could see my son eyes in your eyes and I felt, if my son had lived he would have been a good young man like you. My son had a good heart. He was kind to. He like people, when I would bring him to work with me some time, he would go around and speak to the people in the court house they all knew him and like him they would always have something to give him and he would smile, I loved to see him smile. When I came to see him he would give me a special smile and my heart would melt because I knew he loved me. I never understood why people hate each other because of the color of their skin. When I fell in love with Ethel; all I could see was the good woman she was and how good she was to me. When I make love to Ethel all I could see was a woman I fell in love with. I didn't care what color she was; all I knew was that I loved her. When she told me she was having my baby, I was a happy man and I didn't give a damn what the people in Derry thought. When my son was born, I was right there with Ethel. When that little old wrinkled up baby come in to this world; all I could do was cry and love Ethel even more. Now they gone and I have no one to love. Yes you do Judge, you have me. And I love you for letting Ethel save my Mama in that court room that day. Whenever you need me I will be here for you Judge just call. I loved Ethel too.

When we got to Derry, I took the Judge home and went in with him. He went straight to the bar and had a drink, will you have one with me son? Sure I will. Judge, you Know I don't believe Ethel would want you to give up. You have to keep living as long as you can. You said I remind you of your son, well you still have a son. I'm a black boy too. I may look white, but I came from a black family and I love my family.

My white family loves me just as much. Judge promise me you will take care of yourself. Derry needs you to stay around and be the good Judge you are on the stand. The Judge hugged me and said thank you son. I think you will be hearing from me a lot. Any time Judge, any time.

You have a good trip back home and tell you're Mom and Dad thanks. I'll call them sometimes. Bye Judge. As I was leaving Derry driving back to Oklahoma City I thought about my Mama Cherry Etta where could she be what happen to her why did she leave her kids why did that man mean more to her then her own kids. Katie and I was still living with my Mom and Dad; while our new home was being built. Things were going fine. Harold and my Dad were still getting along fine. Harold had a lot of white friends that liked him but he still wanted to go to the black school. July 24, 1949 Shelly calls me and she was crying. Henry Lee, its grandma she is real sick the ambulance is here and they taking her to the hospital." I'm on my way Shelly. When I get to the hospital I'll call you. After I got to the hospital, I went to the emergency room. I told them I came to see Cora Jackson. Who are you Sir? I'm her grandson. I'm sorry sir we can only talk to her family. I am her family, damn you!

Henry Lee, Henry Lee is that you out there? Yes grandma. Come on in here. I went in; Grandma you okay? I'm a little tired. I know you must be scared; it's the first time you call me grandma. I knew the first time I saw you; I knew you would grow up to be special in my life. Son it's been all most three years now I want you to find your mama for me she is not dead. She is hurt and can't come home to me. Please find my baby. She needs me and I can't help her. When you find her let her know how much I love her." Grandma you can tell her when she come home. No baby; Thomas is calling me to come home with him. My time is up baby. Take care of your sisters and brother until your mama come home. I can't wait until she get here. I wish I could stay and see my grandkid's grown.

Don't talk like that Cora, you will be here for a long

time, I want you to live to help me with my first child. I want my kid's to get to know you. I would love that baby you have to tell them about me. Tell Robert thanks for taking care of Harold and us. I looked at Cora's face and she was grinning. I turned around to see who she was grinning at. It was my Dad standing with my brother and sisters. Dad! Oh Dad! Thank you for coming. I don't know how bad Cora was. Thank you for bringing the kids. Shelly called me to bring them to see Cora, They all kiss Cora and my Dad walked over to her and (said) Cora can I do anything for you? Do you need anything? Robert you and your family have done so much for me, and my family. All I can say is thank you. My dad took Cora by the hand, and said everything will be all right. Cora closed her eyes and died at the age of 79. My Dad took the kids home with him. I stayed and took care of everything and I went home.

My Mom told the girls they could move in with us. They loved Donna like a mother and they wanted to stay with her. Three days later we had Cora's funeral at 5th street Baptist Church at 2: pm. All her friends was there, and they was wondering where was Cherry Etta? I overheard someone said. Oh she is in jail for killing her husband. I could hear so many whispers about Cora's only child and she is not here for her mother's funeral.

I heard a lady say poor, Cora, all she done for that girl. Yes you know Cora had to raise those kids. Well I heard she ran off with old Wayne Moore and he ain't worth a penny. What gone happen to them kids? Some white folks, taking care of them. I was so mad at Cherry Etta, if I knew where she was, I would shake the shit out of her. We took Cora's body to Trice Hill Cemetery, where she was buried beside Grandpa Thomas. Lord what do I do now? What will happen to my black family?

Cora, Thomas, and Cherry Etta are all gone and left these kids for me to take care of. I knew I couldn't ask my Dad and Mom to take care of them. I didn't want to burden my wife with them. What am I going to do I sit there at the cemetery after everyone had gone, I cried, and cried. Why me, why me Lord. Why did you take Cora, where is Cherry Etta Lord, where in the world is she?

Cora why didn't you just leave me alone? You come in my life 22 years later, and 3 years later you die on me. Whenever I find Cherry Etta, if she not dead, I may kill her myself Cora, for leaving you to take care of her kids. What kind of mother just walk away from her family and never call or come back to them? I didn't go home I wanted to be alone to think, so I went to my office. I fix me a drink and I thought about the first time I met Cora coming through my office door. I kept siting there staring at the door looking for Cora to walk in. I fix me another drink and I saw the door coming open. Oh shit! I thought. Cora is that you? As the door opens it was my friend Dean.

Henry Lee is you alright. Yes man you scared the shit

out of me, opening that damn door like that. I thought you were Cora. We both started laughing. You want a drink? Yes make it a double. What you doing here Dean? I came here to be with you, I knew you would be here you always come to your office when you need to think or have a lot on your mind. I wanted to be here with you today. You know I will always be here for you. What can I do to help you to ease your pain? I stood up and put my arms around Dean and told him he have already done more for me than any friend could do. Thank you for being here and for being my friend all these years. After you found out I had a black family. Thank you Dean. We both hug each other and cried like two old ladies.

Come on let's get the hell out of here. You need to go home to your wife and family. Leave your car here and I'll drive you home. Dean drove me home. When we got there I ask him to come in with me and have another drink with me. No man I need to get home, I'll come by tomorrow. If you want to stay home for a few days; I'll take care of everything at the office for you. Okay Dean, thank you. I went into the house and Katie was still waiting up for me. She got up and gave me hug and (said) baby you alright? Do you need me to get you something to eat or drink? No nothing to drink, Dean and I were at the office and we had a few drinks.

Baby I just want to go to bed and try to get some sleep. Katie and I went to bed and I just laid there thinking about Cora and wondering what happen to Cherry Etta. I looked at the clock and it was 1:30 am I fell asleep.

At 5:30 am the phone rings, rings, rings. Hello, (I said) and nobody said anything. I hung the phone up and went back to sleep. Four minutes later the phone ring again. I pick up the phone and a voice (said). Henry Lee don't you hang up that damn phone I ain't in the mood for your shit; you come and get me; this is your Mama Cherry Etta Jackson. I was still half sleep; Cherry Etta is dead. I ain't dead I'm in jail, down here in Oklahoma City, come get me. Cherry Etta is that really you? Hell yes it's me, come get me. What in the hell you doing in jail? You been in there for 3years? No Henry. Well where in the hell you been? They said I have to get off the phone, just come get me.(Katie woke up) Henry is everything all right? Who was that on the phone this time of morning? Cherry Etta, she said she was in jail, wanting me to come and get her. I thought she was dead. Well I guess not. What did she said happen to her? I don't know she had to get off the phone. You want me to come with you? No, call Dean for me while I get dress and tell him to meet me at the jail house. I'll go see what is going on and I'll call you when I found out.

When I got to the police station I ask them what did they have Cherry Etta Jackson charged with and how much was her bond? They said she was charged with prostitution. Her bond was 500, hundred and fifty dollars. When Dean came down I ask him would he get her out I was so mad I didn't want to get her out. Dean took care of everything. We waited until they let her out. She came out just grinning she ran to me and said Henry Lee it's so good to see you. I knew you would come get me. Henry, take me to see mama and the kids I sure miss them. I know mama will be so glad to see me.

I know she is mad at me for not getting in touch with her, but after I tell her what happen she will understand. I want to just hug my kids. Come on Henry what you keep standing there for with that blank look on your face? Is something wrong? You see I ain't dead. Come on, damn it! What you looking at me for as if I done something wrong. Come on I'll take you to see your kids and Mama. Get the hell in the car! Why you being so mean to me, ain't you glad to see me?

Where you taking me way out here in the country for? I heard mama and the kids moved on 8th street. What's wrong with you? Just shut the fuck up, I'm taking you to see your mama first. I didn't say another word to her and she got real quite. Then she (said) if you don't want to help me Henry just say so. You don't have to get all mad. I drove up in the cemetery. Henry, what you bring me to this damn cemetery? I didn't say anything.

Henry Lee are you trying to be funny, I told you I ain't dead. I stop the car and said get out- get out damn you! You heard me get the fuck out now. She got out and I said there is your mama lying there. She looked at me as if I was the damn crazy one. She broke down and cried. She ran over crying; "Mama, mama you in there? She threw herself over her mother's grave. Mama I'm so sorry I wasn't here for you I couldn't help it. I'm so sorry please, forgive me. I went over, picked her up, put my arms around her, and told her to cry all she wanted to I 'm here for you. I took her back to the car.

Henry what happened? When did she die? She died three days ago, and we buried her today. Cora was worried about you the whole time you was gone. We all thought you was dead everyone but Cora. She kept telling me you were alive and needed help. She wanted me to keep looking for you and bring, you back to your kids. Cora died of a broken heart, and bad kidney because of you. I'm so sorry Henry, I'm so sorry. Come on I'll take you to see your kids. But before I do you going to tell me where the hell you been for 3 years? And why you never called to see about your Mama? I couldn't come home, I tried! You don't know how hard I tried. I miss my kids so much and I prayed that one day I could live to come back to them. But that damn man I was with wouldn't let me.

What do you mean? I thought you were so damn bad no other man would ever hurt you again. I can't believe you would let a man keep you from your Mama and kids. I don't want to hear that shit. Henry if I could have I would have. Cherry started to cry. You don't understand son. Tell me so I can understand. I was just going to ride down to Derry to see Ethel and come on back. On our way there we was drinking then my boyfriend started smoking that shit and we started to get high. When we got to Ethel's house she was glad to see me. She cooked and we were having a nice time. Ethel gave me some money before we left. My boyfriend told Ethel he wanted to go to Nebraska.

He was driving the car and he pulled out a joint and we smoked and started back to Oklahoma City. I don't know what happened; I went to sleep. I don't know how we passed Oklahoma City. We got lost and Wayne just kept driving. I asked him where, were we going. He said he was taking me to his house and just sit back and enjoy the ride. By then I was so high, I didn't care where we was. He would stop to get gas and he gave me a pill and I went back to sleep. I woke up and it was dark and I didn't know where in the hell we were. We were getting low of gas and almost out of money and Wayne pulled into this filling station but it was closed. He broke in it and we took some food. Then he opens the cash register, he stole some money out of it and we hurry up and jump back in the car and took off before somebody came by and saw us. We went a little ways down the road and we stop and got gas I stayed in the car.

I didn't' know where I was. He kept driving and the next thing I know we were in Florida. He told me that was where he lived. I told him he needs to take me back home. He took me down a dirt road so far back in the woods. He wouldn't let me go. I pull out my gun and said you son of bitch, take me home. I'm going home. That bastard hit me so damn hard I woke up in a shack, all tied up. He kept me there. He was giving me some kind of pills to make me sleep. I started to spit them at him and he would start beating my ass, so I just kept taking them. He would leave and go to town and came back with food and more pills. He wasn't working and I was wondering where he was getting money to buy food and gas he said he was breaking in people home getting the food and he found some money in a few homes. No one could find him because he was out in the woods. He kept me tied up in one of the bedrooms, when he would leave. I tried and tried to get loose. I didn't know where I was. He took my gun from me.

Henry Lee he would beat me and rape me so much I just didn't give a damn any more. I started to take them pill so much I didn't want to think I just wanted to die. I was hoping he would kill me and stop putting me in so much pain. There wasn't a phone there, all I had to listen to was his sorry ass and a battery radio. I had to cook on a wood stove, we didn't have lights, and we only had candles and oil lamps at night. There wasn't even a bathroom. He gave me a big pot to use and I had to dump it myself. He would say to me you listen to me bitch! You empty your own shit. He follow me in the woods when I had to dump it. I was hopping a bear would come out of nowhere and eat his ass up so I could try to find my way home.

There was a pond not far from the house he would go get water and make me boil it for drinking water. It would be three or four days before he would let me take a bath. He didn't want to keep going to the pond packing water back. I didn't see anybody but him. He was crazy. I got myself in another damn mess I couldn't get out of. I knew one day I would have to try to get away from him. But I didn't know how. He kept me so doped up sometimes I didn't even remember I had a mama and kids. One day he didn't lock me up. He knew he had worn me down. He kept my car keys with him all the time and when he go to sleep he give me those damn pills and I go to sleep too.

"Well that day I woke up before he did and I went outside to run. I didn't know which way to go so I took out running down that damn dirt road as fast as I could. I was running for my life! I was running so fast I never looked back; I knew I was free. But the next thing I knew something hit me. That damn dirty bastard hit me with the car! He tried to kill me when he hit me with the car! I fell to the ground and when I woke up a few days later, he had me tied to the bed and was raping me and I wish he had just killed me. I begged God to let me die that day. He just kept making me take them damn pills. I was so scared of him I didn't try to run anymore. I told him that I would never try to leave him anymore. So I gave up. Cherry Etta started crying so hard I told her to stop and I'll take her to the kids and we would talk more later.

No Henry! I want to tell you everything because I won't ever talk about it again. How did you get away from him? Is he dead? "Yes, yes, yes; his black ass is dead. I will never have to see him again and his black ass will never have to see me or hurt me anymore."

Cherry Etta started laughing and laughing; no one will ever see that black bastard again unless they go to hell to see him. Cherry what did you do? I didn't do a damn thing to him. One morning I laid there tied up and couldn't get out of that damn bed. I started to pray to God to help me I told God I couldn't take it anymore and would he please let me die or will he come help me.

Wayne came in the bed room untied me and said he was going fishing. He locked the bedroom back and I heard him go out the door. I went to the window looking out at him. I saw him with his fishing pole going to the pond down by the house to fish and for some reason, I said to myself; God is this the day I go free? I kept looking out the window at him then a few minutes later I saw him bend over with his ass to the pond. Cherry Etta started laughing and laughing. I thought she was going crazy, then she said; Henry Lee, all of a sudden I saw him turn around and he fell in the pond.

The next thing I know is I saw his black ass just swimming as fast as he could, trying to get to shore. You know how they make you run real fast in a movie? Well his ass was swimming as fast as he could go and just as he was getting out of the water; a damn Alligator bit him in his ass and he went down. I saw that damn gator with his ass in its mouth; that damn gator came back up and all I could see the last of his black ass going down that gator's mouth. I laugh and I laugh, and I laugh. That day, that, old gator come to save my life. God sent him to help me go free.

I got the chair that he sometimes tied me up in and I kept beating on that window until I broke the glass out. I climbed out went around to the door, came back in, and thank God he had left my car keys on the table. I jump my ass in that car and I took off as fast as I could down that dirt road. I was driving so damn fast; all I could see behind me was dust. When I got to the end of that dirt road, there was a highway. I didn't know which way to go. I got on it and just drove. I didn't have money, clothes or nothing to eat. I didn't give a damn I knew I was a free woman. I was so damn happy that old Mr. Gator came to save me after 3 years.

He took his ass down to that pond to fish and he never said he saw a gator in there. When I got on that highway I didn't know where I was going. I just took off driving that damn car as fast as I could; never looking back. Then the damn car started putting' and putting along and then it stopped on the side of the rode, I guess it was out of gas. I didn't know where the hell I was, I just got out and I started walking down the highway. I got about h a l f mile from the car and this man and his wife drove up beside me and the man ask me was I having car trouble? Yes sir, I'm trying to get home to Oklahoma to see my kids.

They told me to get in and they would take me as far as they were going. I told them I was hungry and tired. When they got to a small town in Florida, they stopped and said it was where they were going. The man gave me ten dollars and said "good luck lady" and they drove off. I saw this trucker and ask him where was he going? He told me to Oklahoma! I ask him if I could ride that far with him. "Yes" (he said) get in I be glad just to have someone to talk to. Where you from? Oklahoma (I said.) when I got in that truck, I told him my car broke down. Well I'll take you to Oklahoma.

I was so happy he act like a real nice White man. We was laughing and talking he was telling me about his wife and kids. I told him I had some kids and was on my way to see them. We rode for about one hour and a half and he pull off the road. I said anything the matter? Why we stopping? Well I hope you know you have to pay me for a ride. Sure I just got ten dollars. Will that help take me as for as you can? Ten dollars is not enough for me. Well when we get to Oklahoma I'll tell my son to give you some more money. He is a rich lawyer in Oklahoma City. I don't give a damn, who your, son is I need to get paid right now. He made me get in the back of the truck and he raped me. Then he told me to get my ass out of his truck that was for as he was going.

If I had my gun with me I would have shot his fat ass, then and there. When I run out of Wayne's house I didn't think about getting my gun or a knife. I didn't think nothing else would happen to me. I left my gun in them damn woods and I didn't even have a knife on me. I left quickly. I started to walk again. I was tired and hurt that I ask God 'why did he let all this happen to me? I didn't do nothing wrong to deserve all this. The things I did wrong in my life it was all to protect me or my kids. I walk and walk, God please forgive me for all the wrong I did.

I was so tired my legs hurt and my feet, starting to swell. I was just getting ready to lie down on the side of the highway to rest; when another trucker pulled over and stopped. I didn't know if I ought to just lay there on the highway or get in the truck with another trucker and get raped or maybe this one may kill me and leave me beside the road. I cried out to God and ask him to please help me. The man asked me if I was alright and I said hell naw! I'm tired, I'm hungry and I'm trying to get home to Oklahoma. Come on get in I'm on my way to Kansas, I'm going through Oklahoma."

"Let me tell you one damn thing before I get in this truck. I ain't got nothing and I was just raped by the last trucker I rode with and he kicked me out of his truck after he raped me. He drove off and left me. If you planning on doing the same thing, I rather lay here beside the damn highway and let a car run over my ass. I'm too damn tired for anymore shit. (He said) Lady I can't let you stay out here it's getting dark out here, come on I won't hurt you. Come on get in. So I thought what the hell; it ain't been like I ain't been rape before. So I got in with him and I started to feel safe.

He told me he was a preacher and he drove trucks to make extra money for his family. We stop at a truck stop. He reached for a big c o w b o y h a t, got down out of the truck with cowboy boots on and he look like he was 6' 9. He had light blue eyes and he smiled at me. "What's your name? Cherry Etta. That's a pretty name, just call me Rex. I'll go in and get us something to eat what would you like for me to bring out for you? I don't care just something to eat. I sit in the truck and wait for him to come out. He bought me a big hamburger, fries and a strawberry shake. Boy was it good. Thank you Rex I pray God will bless you for being so kind.

Getting back on the road; he said Cherry you smell real bad. I told him everything that happened to me. He told me he would take me some where I could clean up. I knew then that he wanted me to pay him back with my ass. I thought, preacher or no preacher they all want some ass too. He got a room and told me to go in and take me a bath and that he would wait for me in the truck. I went in the room and then he knocked on the door he talked through the door and said he I bought me a pair of his pants and a shirt. I opened the door and (he said). The pants maybe a little long but you can roll them up. You have a good night sleep Cherry; I'll see you in the morning.

I said to myself; God you did hear my prayers. Thank you, thank you! I locked the door and put a chair under the door knob just in case old Rex changed his mind and wanted to come in before day. After I took a bath, I washed out my panties because I knew they would be dry the next morning. I went to sleep and it felt so good. That was the first time in 3years I had a good night sleep without pills. The next morning Rex knocked on the door; Cherry, Cherry are you awake? It's time for me to go do you still want that ride? I'll be right out Rex. (I said). When I opened the door to come out, he was standing there with a piece of rope in his hand. Oh shit I said to myself not you to Rex; I thought you were a nice guy that maybe God sent you to help me. Cherry I know my pants may not stay up on you I don't have another belt, so you have to tie this rope around you to hold up your pants. Oh thank you God and thank you Rex. We made it to Oklahoma and he put me out on 2nd street. I thanked him and told him I would always keep him in my prayers. When I got to the house Mama and the kids was gone. I didn't know where they were or what happen to them. It was four o'clock in the morning and I didn't want to wake up my next door neighbor. So I walked down on 2nd street because I knew someone would still be out on the street. I was going to ask someone if they knew where they were. I ran into Papa Toad and he told me some white folks came and moved them down on 8th street. He didn't know the address. He told me where they were so I was on my way to see if I could find them. I was standing on the comer to cross the street when the damn police pull up and ask me for I D. I didn't have anything on me, so they push me on the car and said spread wide. And take everything out of my pocket. I told him I didn't have anything and he patted me down anyways.

The officer asked me my name? I told him Cherry Etta Jackson. What you doing out here this time of morning? I'm trying to find my kids. "Don't be funny with me bitch, you know damn well ain't no kids out this time of morning. So I told him to kiss my ass. Then I started to walk away and that, bastard grab me, threw me down to the ground, hand cuff me and told me he was taking my smart ass to jail for prostitution. I wanted to take that damn gun out and shoot his ass. He put me in the car and took me to jail. They booked me and locked me up. I told them I wanted my one call and they act like they didn't hear me and walked off. I told that damn cop to bring his ass back and let me out. I yelled I have been in enough shit the past three years to last me a long damn time and he kept on walking.

I sit there for an hour and he came back and (said) are you ready to make your one call with your smart ass.

I did everything I could to keep my mouth closed. If he said one more thing to me I knew it maybe another hour before I get my call. I call you and you know the rest. Cherry Etta you have to go back to the police and tell them what happen to you and report what happen to Wayne. You have to take the police back to where you were in the woods. They have to tell his family. Henry Lee Wilson, are you a damn fool!!! or are you trying to be funny? I hope you're being funny, because if you think I give a damn if his family knows or not, you wrong. He didn't give a damn about my family when he kept me lock up and tied up for three years from my mama and kids. I ain't going back and show no police where that old Alligator, ate his black ass up.

Do you think you going to find his ass in that gator mouth? If you want to go tell the police you go and you and the police can drive down there to Florida. You all can drive down every damn dirt road till you find him. You have my blessings cause I ain't going no damn where and if you and the police find him in that damn gator mouth tell him I said kiss my ass, because he is right where he belong. If I have to take the police back there it will be to thank old Mr. Gator for freeing my ass. So don't you tell me I have to go back, because I ain't going no damn where. Anyway his Mama, maybe glad his mean ass is gone; she won't have to worry no more.

Cherry what happen to you? You're not the same lady I first met in Derry. The people there said you were nice and they like you. If somebody took your ass to the woods for three years away from your family and treat you like a damn dog would you be nice? I ain't going to be nice to no damn body. Nobody but my kids and I mean nobody. That damn bastard was good for nothing! That Alligator knew his ass was sorry that is why he did his family a favor and ate his ass up. That sorry man kept me from my mama and now he is dead; because of his ass not letting me come home. He changed me to become a bitter ass bitch, Tommy, that damn trucker that was mean to me, help change me and all the sorry ass men that hurt me and your damn, daddy is there with them.

Cherry I have to tell the police what happen. Well you go right ahead if it makes you feel better, If you think the police is going to try to find his ass, you be my guess. But let me tell you one damn thing; I ain't going back! You do what you have to do because I don't give a damn. Why you looking at me like that? Take me to my kids now, do you hear me?" I'm taking you to your kids and I want you to stay away from me. I'm tired of you! From now on you do what the hell you want! Do you hear me? Yes I do hear you. I can take care of myself from now on. I called Donna to let her know we were coming, so she would be up when we got there. When we got to the house Donna had the door open and she was standing there for us to come in. Donna this is Cherry Etta. Hello Miss Jackson, I stay here with your girls and I took care of your mother before she died. "Thank you". What do you mean you take care of my girls? Where is Harold? Henry Lee where is my son? He is with me. The girls wanted to stay with Cora. Harold wanted to stay with us.

Well I'm home now; you can bring him back with me. You just rest and we will talk tomorrow. Shelly and Carrie heard Cherry Etta's voice and came in the room. Cherry saw them and just started screaming; "My babies! My babies! She ran to them and just started kissing on them. Look at you Shelly, you are so beautiful and Carrie you look like an angel. My babies are all grown up. Shelly's eyes was so big, she said I thought you was dead. No baby I'm not dead. Carrie started to cry and ran to Donna. Shelly (said) where you been mama? Why you didn't come home? Why did you leave us? Grandma was so sad all the time worrying about you. Couldn't you have just called her and let her know you were not dead? She died because she wanted you home with us. She thought you was hurt and couldn't come home."

Baby I was hurt. If I could have come home I would have. I thought about all of you every day. I cried every day that I was not home with you. Were you with a man? Shelly we will talk about that later. Oh baby you sure have grown. Baby I won't ever leave you again. I'm here to stay. Thank you, Henry Lee for moving my mama and kids in this nice house. You bring Harold tomorrow. Thank you too Donna for taking care of my family. I can do it now. Mr. Wilson, Do you want me to leave now? No Donna, we will talk about it tomorrow. Shelly and Carrie said "No! Donna is not going anywhere. This is her home too and she stays with us. We love her! She, been our mama for three years and she stays or we leave with her. I could tell by the look on Cherry's face she wanted to say something, but she just smiled.

I told them all to go back to bed and get a good night sleep and everything will be all right the next day. I left and went home. When I got home, Katie woke up. "Henry what happened? What took you so long? I told Katie everything that happened. I knew I had to face Mom and Dad, to tell them Cherry wanted Harold back with her. I don't know what Dad will say. Dad and Mom love Harold and I know they don't want to give him up. When I got up and went down for breakfast, everyone was already there eating breakfast. Good morning Henry (mom said). Everyone else said, good morning."

I tried to smile but my dad said what's wrong with you? Had a bad night? Katie what wrong you not taking good care of your man? Katie looked funny and dropped her head. I tried to eat but Dad kept looking at me. I know he knew something was wrong. I never was good at hiding things from him.

Henry Lee what the hell wrong with you? I know you got something on your mind let it out. Dad I need to tell you and mom, something. I got a call last night from Cherry Etta. She is alive and I picked her up from the police station last night. She is at the house with the girls. Harold (said) is she alright? Where have she been? Why did she stay away so long?

She said she was in Florida and she couldn't call from where she was because she didn't have a phone. Was she in prison for three years? Harold she wants to see you. She wants you to come home with her and the girls. My dad said Hell no! Harold is not moving in with her. She left him and I been taking care of him. Dad he is her son and she have the right to take him back. Harold said I don't want to go back I like it here I love you Pops! Please don't let me go back to her. You don't have to Harold. Get ready and I will take you to school. Dad you have to let her see him. I don't have to do a damn thing. Cherry Etta can go back to where ever she came from for all I care. Come on son let's go. Dad took Harold and left. I ask mom what she thought. Henry, your dad and I love Harold and we don't want to give him up. Your dad is going to put up a fight for him.

Mom, Cherry wants to see him and I don't think she is going to give him up either. She do, love her kids. Dad has to let her see him. Henry Lee you know your dad. He does things the way he wants to. She will have a hard time getting Harold from him. Well I have to get to the office. Katie walk, me to the door. Honey, what can I do to help? Nothing I will try to think of something. I kiss Katie and told her thanks for caring; I'll call you after I get to work. I love you for being you and putting up with my family. When I got to the office the phone was ringing. Mr. Wilson you have a call from Cherry Etta Jackson. She said she will not hang up and don't put her on hold and if I hang up she will keep calling., if I don't put you on the phone she will be down here to kick my ass and make sure you fired me. What do you want me to do?

I'll take it. What do you want now, Cherry Etta? I want to know when you bringing Harold home. I'll bring him after he gets out of school. Did you and Donna get along? Did the girls go to school this morning? "I ain't seen my baby in three years and I want to see him with me today. I know you don't want me to act a fool." I said I will bring him and I will. I'm very busy I can't talk to you for the rest of the day, you have to wait. An hour later, the phone rings. It was the school. Mr. Wilson there is a Cherry Etta Jackson here saying Harold is her son and she wants to pick him up from school. Harold is crying and saying she ain't his mother and that his mother is dead. What do I do? I didn't want to go to the school. I was getting tired of Cherry Etta doing whatever she wanted. I know she love and want to see her son but look like just a few more hours, she could waited.

I went to the school and Cherry Etta was sitting outside on the curb, crying. I parked the car and told her to get in and stay till I come back. I went into the school and went in the office and when Harold saw me he ran to me. Henry Lee, mama was here to get me. I don't want to go with her. I love where I am. Henry, I have seen so many people having fights, shooting people, Mama walking the streets and I don't want to live like that ever again. I am scared at night. I can hear the people next door cussing at each other and where I am now, is all good. Harold your mama just wants to see you. She's been gone for three years and she missed you. Maybe if she can just talk to you and you let her know you happy where you are now; then maybe that is all she wants to know. Will you just talk to her? It will make you feel better if you do. Ok Henry, I'll see her but I'm not going home with her. She left me and never called or came to see me and now that she's back she wants to see me.

I check Harold out of school and when we got to the car, Cherry Etta was gone. You see Henry, she gone again. I 'm tired of her running off. Will you please take me home? Harold and I went home. When we got home Dad, wanted to know what was wrong with Harold. Why you home? Did something happen at school? Yes.´ Harold what have you done? Nothing! Harold go to your room while I talk to Dad. What's wrong son? Cherry Etta came to the school to pick up Harold, he didn't want to leave with her and he started crying; saying she was dead and she was not his mama. That damn woman!

I went over on 8th street to see why Cherry Etta left. Donna said Cherry Etta was drunk and she had to help her get into bed. Some of her friends had bought her home. Do you want me to go wake her? No Donna, just leave her alone. Donna don't you take any crap off her! Just tell her how you feel because you are not her maid and you don't have to do nothing for her. Let her do it herself. Make her help you with the girls and make the girls help you too. I don't have any trouble out of the girls, they are good girls. If you need anything Donna, call me or Mom. I will Mr. Wilson. Good bye. Three days pass and I didn't hear nothing from Cherry Etta. Wednesday Donna called and said, Mr. Wilson, I'm leaving Friday to go to Texas. My sister is sick and I will be gone for a few days. If she is better I will be back by Monday. You will have to check on the girls because Cherry Etta doesn't always come home every night and when she do she's been drinking. Okay Donna I'll have mom come and pick them up after school.

I called Shelly and she said her mom wasn't home. Shelly if she's not there by five o' clock call me. I called Mom and told her that I would be late coming home and would she pick the girls up for me. She said, she, Dad, and Harold were going to the lake for the weekend. But she would go get the girls and leave them with Katie. The girls wanted to go with Harold to the Lake. So I told Mom wait for me and I would go too. When I got home Katie said she was going. We all packed and went to the lake. Mom said she left Cherry Etta a note and told her the girls were with us for the weekend, and Donna was gone to Texas.

The kids love the lake. Dad, Harold, the girls and I went on the boat fishing. Mom and Katie stayed and cooked. It was so nice at the lake it was so peaceful and quiet there. I loved it there too. The kids were having so much fun. Dad had a tree house built up there when I was a kid. Dean and I spent a lot of time in the tree house, talking about what we were going to do when we grew up and about girls. We got back late Sunday evening. I called Cherry Etta to tell her I was bringing the girls home but there was no answer. I waited and called back and she still didn't answer. I told the girls to spend the night and I would take them to school on my way to work. I called back at 9:pm and she still didn't answer! I wondered where she was.

Donna said she had found her another boyfriend. Cherry Etta was mad at Donna because she wouldn't let him move in or spend the night with her. So she sometimes stays with him. The next morning I drop the kids off to school and I went on to work. Around 10: am, my secretary said, someone was on the phone crying and wanted to talk to me. She said it sound like Donna.

Hello. Henry Lee, Henry Lee, you have to come quick, it's your mama!" What the hell have she done now? I think she is dead and the kids don't need to come home, its blood everywhere! What happen? I don't know! I found her on the bed! I didn't touch her! Do you want me to call the police? I 'm on my way! When I got to the house, Donna was sitting on the porch. When I drove up in the driveway she ran to me, crying. Donna stay out here. I went in the house and Cherry Etta was lying on the bed with blood all over her. Oh my God! What in the world happened? I called the ambulance and I waited outside with Donna.

When they got there they wanted to know what was wrong. I told them the lady in the house was dead she wouldn't move. The police came up and wanted to know what was going on? They went in the house and one of the officers came out and said, she was barely alive, she look like she was beat almost to death and that someone was trying to kill her. They ask Donna if she knew what happened and she said she had just got back home from Texas. She came home early because she wanted to be home when the girls got home from school, and found t h e i r   m o t h e r in the house and that she didn't see anyone else in the house when she got home. The police ask me why was I there. I told them Donna called me because I was part of their family. I still didn't tell people I was her son. She did that for me and nobody believes her.

The police asked a lot of questions then they went next door and ask people if they saw anyone or heard anything? The lady said, she heard someone screaming and she looked out the door and it stopped. So she just shut the door and she didn't see nothing or hear nothing else. I learned that some blacks won't tell you anything. They stick together; they don't like to get involved. After the police, left we locked the house up, and I told Donna to come home with me. We went by the school and picked the girls up before they heard about their mother. When I went in to pick Shelly up, we were walking down the hall and a little girl asked Shelly where you going with that white man? You did something wrong? This is my brother. Girl, you need to stop lying! He white and you black. I turn around and said I am her brother. Do you have a problem with that?

When we got to the car and Shelly saw Donna; she was so happy to see her. She gave Donna a long tight hug. Why are you guys picking me up from school so early? What have mama, done now? She ran off again? Or did she kill someone else? No Shelly. Donna went in and got Cherrie, she wanted to know why we were picking her up so early. What was wrong? Your mother is sick and had to go to the hospital. I'm going to drop you off with Harold and I will go see how she doing. When I get there, I can tell you more. I told Shelly to tell Dad and Mom I will call them after I got to the hospital. "Henry Lee, I'll go to the hospital with you. You don't have to Donna. Yes, I want to. When we got to the hospital Cherry Etta was in surgery. I gave them all the information they needed to know about her. I told them don't worry about the bill and that I would take care of it. Donna and I sat in the waiting room. I waited almost an hour and then I went to the desk and asked the nurse if she knew what was going on? "The doctor will come and talk with you sir, she is still in surgery. I called home and Dad answered the phone. Henry Lee, what in the hell wrong with your Mama now? I told Dad she had been beaten almost to death and that Donna found her when she came home. "Is she gone die or is she already dead? She is still in surgery and I don't know anything right now. Son is you alright? You need me to come be with you? No Dad, Donna is here. Just take care of the kids for me and tell them not to worry. What hospital she in? She's at University. Ok son, call me back when you know something.

Two hours later the doctor came out and said Cherry would be alright. She was in recovery and we could see her when they put her in a room. He said they had to put thirty stitches in her head and her wrist was broken. Her face was swollen real big it looks like she was trying to protect her face and threw her arm up and she had to have ten stitches on her lips. Whoever did this to her; beat her on the head with something mighty heavy. He looked at Donna and said your daughter will have to have a lot of care. Her head and face is swollen so bad we have to wait to see when the swelling go down to see if she has any brain damage. She was barely alive when she was brought into the hospital and she had lost a lot of blood. Mrs. Jackson, I'm sorry about your daughter. Her face is messed up real bad and it will be a long time before she start, looking the same. Do you have any questions to ask me? Donna said "No.

I just stood there in the waiting room, I couldn't say anything. I just had tears running down my face. The doctor said she must mean a lot to you. Are you a good friend? No. She is my mother. The doctor looked funny as if he didn't understand. I know he wanted to know what I was talking about. Donna put her arm around me while I cried. The doctor said he would send a nurse to come for us. Donna and I were waiting for the nurse to come back and get us to go see my mama. I was so tired of getting her out of so much trouble. I couldn't understand why she wouldn't listen to me. I look up and in walks Dad and Katie.

Katie came to me and hugged me. "Henry I 'm sorry about your mother, is she going to be all right?" The doctor said she would be. We are waiting for someone to come for us. I said Dad please don't say anything, before he could say anything the nurse walks in and said Cherry Etta is in her room and we could see her. When I walk in to see her, her face it was swollen so big I didn't know her. My Dad asks the nurse if she was going to be all right. He said straight out tell me the truth!" "Sir, she was beaten real badly on her head and face. We really don't know if she can remember what happened to her until the swelling goes down. You have to talk to her doctor. Dad will you take Katie and Donna home? Take Donna home with you. She doesn't need to go back to the house until it's been cleaned. Ask Mom if she knows a good cleaning service that can come out to clean the house. I don't want the girls to see all that mess.

Did you tell the kid's what happen? I told them someone broke in the house and their mom had to go to the hospital because she was hurt. They didn't want to come. Henry Lee I'm staying here with you. You don't need to be alone. I'll be all right Katie. You heard what I said, I'm staying! Dad and Donna left. Cherry Etta was still sleep. So Katie and I went to get us some coffee. While we were sitting there I heard some nurse say they bought a black woman in and she was almost beat to death they don't know if she is going to live. Someone tried to kill her. I wonder what she did to them. She will be lucky if she lives." Before I could say anything Katie caught me by the arm and said honey please don't say nothing to them.

Cherry Etta stayed in the hospital almost two months. When she came home, she needed help to get around. I made sure the police found the man that did it to her. When they picked him up; he was down on 2nd street drunk and they took him to the station. I told them I wanted to be there when they questioned him. He said he took Cherry home and walked her to the door. He knew he couldn't go in because that damn woman that took care of h e r kid's wouldn't let him in. He told her bye and walked off the porch.

He said, when he got to the side walk Cherry came to the door and called him back. (He said) Cherry said that I could come in and that no one would be home for the whole week end. She had found a note that they left for her. I went in and I was telling her what a nice house she lived in and I wondered how could she pay for it because she don't work? She said she had a rich son that took care of her He went on telling the story about how Cherry told him her son told the maid to tell him everything on her cause she drink a lot and didn't want to spend all of her money because she had to have the maid take care of everything or he would cut off all her money and that was the only reason she let the damn maid stay so she can get her money.

"We laughed about it. Then she went in the kitchen and she cooked me and her some dinner. We went to her room and man she had bottles of whisky hid in her room. I mean whatever I wanted to drink. She said the maid didn't come in her room and that she was not allowed to come in her room, but she had to keep it clean or the maid would tell her son. We got drunk, I made love to her, and the next morning when I woke up, we started back to drinking. We was just laughing and playing around. I told her to go fix me some of her good breakfast and serve it to me in bed. I went in the kitchen to see what was taking her so long because I didn't smell no breakfast cooking.

She was sitting at the table drinking, Cherry where is my breakfast? Get your ass up and cook." She looked at me and said fuck you! The last two damn men that told me to cook for them is dead and I ain't cooking for any more damn men. She got up, threw a drink in my face, we got to cussing and she reached over and got a butcher knife and came at me. I told her to put it down but then she cut me on the arm. When I saw the blood running down my arm I just lost it. I saw the skillet on the stove, I picked it up and she came at me again with the knife still in her hand. I was just going to hit her on her hand so she could drop the knife. I don't know what happened to me, I just kept hitting her and hitting her. I saw blood all over her and I got scared. I ran out the door; when I got outside I went behind the house and I still had the skillet in my hand. I ran down the alley and dropped it in a trash can."

I called my brother and he picked me up and took me to Spencer Oklahoma. I stayed out there for a week and the police didn't came for me, I thought she was alright, so I came back to town today. I didn't mean to hurt her and I am so sorry. I really didn't mean to hurt her. They told me at the bar that she was beat to death and the police was looking for me. When I ran out the bar to go back to my brother's house, the police was waiting outside and picked me up. I told them I didn't mean to kill her. I loved her. I looked at this sick man and wanted to kill him myself. I told them I didn't want him out of jail until he go to court and for them to file charges on him for Cherry Etta.

I knew she would need a lot of help; so I hired

someone to come in and take care of her. It was enough for Donna to take care of the girls. I told Donna the lady I hired was only to care for Mama. Cherry Etta was not the same; sometimes she couldn't remember things and there were times I thought she was putting on an act. So we all felt sorry for her. One day I stopped by there to see how things were, and mom's car was there. I wondered what she was doing there. I parked the car and when I walked on the porch I could hear Cherry Etta's mouth just going. I just stood there to hear what she was saying. I heard her say, you two mother fuckers looking at me like I 'm crazy. Well I'm not, I'm just sick of everybody treating me like I'm a damn fool.

"I been mistreated ever since Robert bought me to this sorry ass town, I wish I had stayed in Mississippi; all I would have had to do was stay on the plantation and say yes sir and no sir, yes ma'am and no ma'am. Robert dump me for your fat white ass and then you gone have nerve enough to take my two son from me. If you had kept your ass away from him everything you got could have been mines. You done turned my baby against me, well you can't turn my Henry Lee way from me he love me."

I heard Mom say, Cherry that is not true, you're doing it all by yourself. I been nothing but nice to you and your kids. How, can you say that to me? Well bitch I can say whatever the hell I want to. Robert and I were happy in Mississippi, he was good to me, and he was mines first. I had his first baby. He loved me until you came along and took him from me and my kid's should be living in that big house you got. You and Robert bought your ass in here and bought Donna here and she took my girls from me. They won't listen to a damn thing I say, they run and ask her black ass. Then God took my Daddy and my Mama and I didn't get to say good bye to her because of some damn s t u p I d a s s m a n. Well I'm tired of everybody taking from me.

I don't have anybody to love me. Somebody is always mistreating me. Well damn it no more! I'm going to show you two bitches who going to do the taking. I walk in. Cherry that is enough. Mom what are you doing here? I had the cook to cook enough food to bring over to this house so Donna wouldn't have to cook dinner today. Well ain't that a bitch (Cherry said). Cherry Etta, you may be my mama but you damn sure ain't my mother and if I ever hear you say anything bad to my mother and Donna again, your ass is mines. You disappeared for three years and if you do anything to them; believe me, your ass will disappear for a life time do you understand me? Mom thank you for what you did. I don't want you to give her one more damn thing and I don't want you over here anymore.

Henry Lee, she said she brought the food over here for Donna. What about me? The food was for everyone, Donna just didn't have to cook today. Henry Lee, I've had enough from this woman I don't have to listen to her. I'm out of here. Good take your black ass out of here I'm sick of you too (Donna said). Well Donna, let her go because I'm tired of her. Let her do what the hell she wants. You listen to me Cherry you don't put your damn hands on Donna; if you want to leave you leave. Before you leave I will pick your ass up at 10:00 o'clock in the morning to take you to court. After that you do what the hell you want. You better be here and ready. Now go to your room and leave Donna alone. Come on Mom let's go home.

When we was walking out the door, the girls was coming home and they ran to Mom and gave her a big hug. "Why are you here today, something happening to mama again? No babies, I just came by. Hi Henry Hi girls. They said "we love you Becky" and Henry. "We love you too." They waved as we drove off. Mom went home and told Dad what happened and what Cherry said to her. Mom and Dad tell each other everything. Dad (said) Henry I think it's time your mama went back to Mississippi. I'm not going to stand by and let her talk to Becky like that. Becky have been nothing but nice to her and her whole family. Now it's time I step in and take care of Cherry's ass; she done gone too far."

Dad I told Mom to stay away from her and not to go back over there. From now on, anything need to be done I'll go and her damn ass won't like it when I come. No

Dad you stay away too. No need you getting in trouble. You were right, wish I had listened to you. I should never listen to Cora either. After she go to court tomorrow I'm through with her too. I can't take any more from her. The next morning I went over to pick Cherry up for court. The girls wanted to know why I was over there. I told them I was taking Cherry to court to identify the man that was in the house. I asked Shelly if she wanted to go. No Henry Lee, I got enough of court when mama shot daddy. I don't want to go near another court room.

Cherry didn't say anything. When we got in the car, I asked her why did she say the things to Mom and Donna they had been nice to her. I been nothing but nice to you. I know you been hurt but you don't have to take it out on people who is trying to help you. I have stood by you in all the stupid ass shit you been through, said, and did. One thing I will not stand from you and that is the way you talk to my mom or the way you treat her. My Dad can take care of himself with you. You can act as crazy as you want, if you ever talk to my mother like that again, I will kick your ass, mama or not, do you understand me? She sit there and never said one word to me, just looked out the window.

When we got to the court house, I told her to get up there and tell them how she was beat up and left for dead. I told her that Dean was her lawyer and he will do everything for her.

That it was his case and he was just as good as I

was. She still wouldn't say anything. Cherry, are you all right? Do you hear me? "Yes, I hear." When we got in the court room and they brought Bruce Fisher out; he looked at Cherry and said I 'm sorry. Tears started to run down her face. She still had her arm in a cast and cuts still on her face but a lot of the swelling was gone. When Dean called Cherry to the stand, she sit there. I said, Get up! You hear them, they calling your name. She got up and walk to the stand.

Cherry Etta Jackson do you swear to tell the truth and nothing but the truth so help you God. She stood there and said nothing. She had a very sad look on her face and then she started to scream, and scream, and she got louder, and louder. Then tears started coming down her face. I got up and ran to her. Dean asked for a recess until she was calm. We took her in one of the rooms. Dean was so nice to her; he got her a drink of water and told her to calm down. We all thought when she saw Bruce that it scared her. Dean said Cherry are you scared of him? What's wrong? She was still crying, Cherry are you scared Bruce will hurt you again? Please stop crying and talk to me. Do you want to come back another day? No Dean, I was r e m e m b e r I n g the last time I was in court was for killing my kids daddy for trying to rape my Shelly and beating me. I thought that I saw him in that court room that is why I screamed.

Well Cherry, do you think you can go back in there and just answer a few question for me and we will put

Bruce away so he will never hurt you again? If you let him walk out of there he will do it to another woman and next time he may kill her. He will never beat on you or anyone else. It's up to you. He will get some time anyway because he confessed to the police; we need you to answer the questions I ask you. Will you go back in there for me? Yes Dean, I'll do it for you." We went back in the court room and the Judge wanted to know if she was alight. Dean told him "yes." Cherry Etta was recalled back to the stand. Dean ask her if she was alright. "Yes. Cherry Etta do you see the man in the court room that beat you? Yes. Can you point him out to me? She pointed to Bruce; he dropped his head, and (said) I'm sorry Cherry. You know I love you I didn't mean to hurt you. The Judge told him to "keep quiet."

Dean asked Cherry can she tell him why he hit her. Because I wouldn't cook for his ass and I told him I was tired of men trying to make me do whatever they want. Then he tried to kill me." She started back crying and Dean told the court he didn't have any more questions for her. The court didn't have any questions for her since he had already confessed, he was guilty. Bruce didn't want to go on with the court either. Bruce Fisher was sent to prison for 9 years, for attempted murder without parole. I thanked Dean and told him I would take her home. (She said), No. She wanted Dean to take her home. I took the rest of the day off and went home. I told Katie I wanted to spend the day with her, we went shopping and to lunch.

Around six o'clock that evening, Donna call and ask me how things went in court with Cherry Etta. I told her what happened. I ask her how Cherry was doing. She said she didn't know, Cherry had not come home. She told me the lady next door said she saw Dean drop Cherry off and before Cherry went into the house she saw her get in the car with some man and they drove off. Maybe she will be home later Donna. The next day Donna called back and said Cherry never came home. I don't know where she is. Donna I'm not going to worry about her any more. I told Donna, Cherry is on her own now and don't worry about her, just take care of the girls and I'll call you tomorrow. I fixed me a drink and went to bed early.

I was wondering where she could be. I knew after the beating she took on her head that she wouldn't be able to think good or even say whatever she wanted to. Or whatever she felt like saying something crazy to? Where in the world did she go and who was she with? Well this time I'm not spending money trying to find her she is on her on. I have done a lot for her by taking care of her mama and her kids too. She never acted like she appreciated any of it so to hell with her.

When I got to the office the next morning, Dean was already there. Hi Henry, how did everything go? Fine, Katie and I had a nice time we went shopping and lunch it was good to get away. I'm going to get my life back together before I met Cherry Etta. What do you mean?" Cherry Etta have disappeared again. She never told anyone, like she did before. I don't know if she is hurt or not. Dean I'm worried about her. "Don't be Henry, she is alright." I hope so Dean. "Really man she is fine, I know where she is, she asked me not to tell anyone. She didn't want you to worry about her anymore so she went to be on her own. Henry, she wants to be left alone. I went to see her and I gave her a car to go back and forth to work and enough money to help her get things together. Just leave her alone. It is what she wants." Good I won't bother her. I was tired anyway. I told her to call me if she needs anything. Thank you Dean.

It's been two months and Dean, haven't said where she we r e and I got busy with my cases, my mind was on them and I could think so much better. Mom was feeling better, she had lost a lot of weight and she was happy. When I got home from work, Katie gave me a big hug and kiss. What is all this for? (She said) because I love you. We went in our room she was smiling so. Baby why you look so happy? "Well Henry you look like you could have something in your life to smile about and I think I can make you smile and happy for a long time." Baby I sure could use something. What you got? She came over to me and took my hand and put it on her belly, and said you going to be a daddy I couldn't believe it. Oh Katie, are you for real? Katie told me she was going to have a baby in seven months. She was already two months. I was so happy; Dad and Mom were happy when we told them. They were happier than they have been in a long time. The girls and Harold was happy they were going to be aunts and uncle. Mom couldn't wait to be a grandma. I called Barbara and she came home to stay for a few months to help mom.

It's been seven months and Katie had a little girl. She was born September 23, 1953 and we named her Anna Jean Wilson. She was a beautiful baby; everyone in the house knew she brought so much joy around the house. A week later Shelly was graduating out of high school we all got ready and went to her graduation. After we all sat down, I thought about Cherry Etta not being there. She didn't want us to be in her life anymore. I felt bad that she was missing out on her daughter's graduation and didn't even know she had a granddaughter. I felt she was being selfish.

Shelly acted as if she didn't care because she loved Donna so much. Donna is the one who has been there for her. Donna is the one who told her all the things that a mother should tell her daughter and went to all the things she did at Douglass school. When they called Shelly's name and before we all could stand to clap for her; my God I heard this loud screaming. "Shelly! Shelly! Wow! Wow!" The scream was so loud Shelly just stopped, and looked. It was Cherry Etta. I could tell Shelly was glad she was there and I was glad she came too.

I could tell she had been drinking but she looked good and was dressed real nice. After she came over to us, she hugged Harold and Carrie, and said hello "Henry, I heard I have a grandbaby." She went over to Katie to see the baby. I could tell Katie didn't want her to hold the baby because she was a little tipsy but Katie let her hold her. She said "Hi cutie, this is your grandma Cherry. You are so cute. You look just like your grandma Cora." No one said anything because Anna was white as Katie and me. When Shelly came out, Cherry gave Katie back the baby and ran to Shelly. "Mama is so proud of you. I got you something." This man walked over with a big box, and handed it to Shelly. "Thank you. Oh this is my boyfriend Bill, he drove me here. Mom and Dad didn't say anything to her and she act like she didn't see them. I wanted to tell her off but this was Shelly's night and I didn't want to say anything to start a mess.

I ask Dad and Mom should I ask her to join us for dinner we were having dinner at the house out by the pool. Shelly and Carrie love to come over and play in the pool with Harold. I hired someone to decorate the house and Donna invited some of Shelly's friends over for the party. Dad said "Hell no! Her ass still crazy and she ain't change one bit. If I have to sit there and look at her ass over the table; I think I would throw up on her ass." Mom said "Robert, don't be like that.

Cherry never said anything to Donna. She put her arms around her three kids and said, "Shelly, Bill and I want to take you kids out to eat. I know you guys like Edmondson on 8th street down from the house. I was telling Bill about all that good soul food." Harold said "No we going with Henry and our family. It was already planned and we didn't know you were coming. Shelly said" I'm sorry I want to go with Henry Lee. I said Cherry you and your friend can come with us if you like. No Henry, Bill has his heart set on eating at Edmondson. She went over to Shelly and said "I'll see you later tomorrow before I leave. I would like to have all of you come to visit with me. Shelly since you finished, school you can come live with me now.

Your old friends ask about you and they will love to see you. My old friends what friends? You mean you been in Derry for a whole year and you couldn't

Come to see us or call and let us know where you were? Honey I wanted to get myself together before I let you all, know where I was. I got myself together and I got my job back at the bus station. Now I'm even living in the house Miss Ross left us. I got it fixed up real nice; so I thought you kids wanted to move back to Derry with me. I couldn't believe what I was hearing. My Dad looked at me and said "Go head say everything you want to its okay with me. Or do you want me to, I am not scared." I was just getting ready to say what I wanted to say to her when Mom and

Katie said "No! Not here and not tonight. Let Shelly be happy." Then Shelly said, you said you were trying to change and get yourself together but you doing the same thing all over. You left us a year and were only in Derry. You didn't come see us or call and you think I want to come live with you in Derry. No thank you!" Shelly went over to Donna and hugged her and said "I am ready to go."

I was happy Shelly (said) what she said to her. Cherry said Shelly I told Dean where I was and he knew. I don't know why he didn't tell all of you. Shelly turned around and said Dean is not your kids." I heard Cherry say "See Bill I told you these damn white folks and that black ass witch turned my kids on me." We all got in the Limo and drove off. When we got to the house, some of the kids was already there and some of Harold's friends too. Shelly was surprised. I told Shelly we were going in the house and that it was up to her to keep her friends in line and if things got out of hand come get us. The kids were nice they were just glad to have a pool party.

I saw Dad looking out there at the kids and I really think he liked it; having the noise and laughter around the house. Mom was happy too. After a little over three hour some of the kid's started to leave. They said they had to be home at a good time. After all the kid's left the house from the party, Shelly (said) thanks all of you for such a nice time. I will never forget any of you. Thank you, Mr. Wilson. My Dad said) Shelly I think it's time you and Carrie Marie call me Pop like Harold. I would love that. Shelly came over and gave him, Mom, Katie, and me big hugs. Thank you Henry Lee, for being my brother I will never forget all the things you have done for all of us.

Harold and Carrie came and hugged me too and said we love you too Henry Lee. I couldn't keep it in, so the tears just started to run down my face. Katie said Shelly open your gifts; we want to see what all you have. Shelly opened Mom and Dad's gift first. It was a check for ten thousand dollars. Her, e yes got so big she keep standing there still like a statue. Harold (said) what's wrong with you? Say something." She started to cry and (said) Pop, Mom I can't take this check, it's too much and you have done so much for us. My Dad said that check is for you to go to college. I want you to grow up to be a smart young lady who knows how to take care of yourself and one day help others. Thank you so much, I promise I won't let you down.

Come on Shelly open Henry Lee and Katie's present. Shelly wanted a pair of leather boots that she saw when she and Katie went shopping; we gave her a check also for ten thousand dollars for school. She thanked us and gave us a hug. Then Shelly opened Donna's gift and Donna had bought her new clothes and some jewelry. Harold said. Now Shelly open your mama's present, the best for last." He and Carrie went over and stood beside her to see. When she opened the box; Harold and Carrie, started laughing and laughing. Shelly looked as if her mama had just slapped her across the face. Harold fell to the floor and Carrie was still laughing. I said what is it? Shelly pulled out this dress and started laughing and then she cried. Carrie Marie said it was one of their mama's dresses.

One day she had it on and ask Shelly, how she looked and Shelly told her; "Oh you look real good you look so nice in it; you need to wear it every day. I just love it on you. I just love that dress. Carrie said she and Shelly went in their room and laughed, and laughed. She look like a fool in it. Shelly was being funny. She hated the dress and didn't have the heart to tell mama to put it in the trash. It was a blue dress with a lot of small white flowers all over it with lace around the neck line and sleeves. Mom started to laugh and then we all started to laugh. Katie said "You guys shouldn't laugh. Cherry thought Shelly loved the dress and wanted to give it to her." The kid's looked at Katie and started laughing again. I think it made Katie a little mad because her face turned red.

Dad told Donna and the girls to spend the night, and have breakfast with us. The next morning we all got up and we all decided to go to church. After church, Dad said "We better take you girl's home, your mama is probably mad as hell and it ain't no telling what she might do." Donna wanted to stop and pick up some chicken and she said she would cook something to go with it. We got enough for us too because our servants was off on Sundays. When, we drove up to the house. Cherry and her boyfriend was backing out of the drive way. Cherry looked mad (Dad said). Henry, look like Cherry, going to kick you and Donna ass. Everyone started to laugh. Donna said I know she crazy but not that damn crazy. The girls got out of the car and said hi Mama where you going?

I'm on my way back to Derry. I just stopped by to tell you all good bye. Where in the hell you been I came by last night and nobody was home. I just came back and no one was home. I put a note on the door. I thought you all didn't want to say good bye to me. Shelly said, oh mama we didn't know you were coming by last night but we here now. Come on in. (Shelly said) Donna, do you mind if Mama, have dinner with us. No' I don't mind. I could see the look on Donna's face looking like she wished her ass would have said no. Cherry said Henry, will you; Harold, Katie and the baby have dinner with me? Dad said he would send the driver back for us him and Mom went home. They didn't want to stay. Mom said go on Henry, she be leaving after a while and you haven't seen her in almost a year. She's been a good girl and she hasn't bothered us. Dad said yes go on, maybe it will be another y e a r before we see her ass again.

Katie handed the baby to Shelly as we got out of the car. Shelly wouldn't let Cherry hold the baby until we got inside. Katie told Donna she would help her in the kitchen while we visited. We all went to the living room, and I said, Bill, how long have you known Cherry? She jumped in and said, Now don't you go asking him a lot of questions? I know him when I first moved to Derry. I said Cherry, have you seen Judge Reid since you've been back? I need to call him. Now, why did you ask me that? No, I ain't seen him. I don't have any reason to. I work every day and I go home, and stay. Well good. I'm glad you doing so well. Yes! I'm doing good I have me a good man now that helps take care of me. I called Dean and he helped me get my money after Ethel died. I fixed up the house and Bill helped me put on another bed room if the kids wanted to come see me sometimes if some people let them."

Cherry anytime the kid's want to come see you; I will bring them, you know that. "Well I'd like for my grandbaby to get to know me. Maybe you and Katie will bring her and leave her with me a few days. I look around and saw Katie's face and I knew that wasn't happening any time soon. Katie said "Come on the food is ready." We all went to the dining room table. It was quiet for a second. Cherry said "You girls put your foot in this food. It sure is good, ain't it Bill." He said, "Yes! The food is real good. Cherry you need to learn to cook like this. Well I don't see you turning down what I do cook." Bill kind of laughed. I didn't say much at the table. I wanted to eat and go. Then Cherry said, Yes, Dean been helping me with all the things I need and I told him he was my lawyer so I want everything k e p t between us. He ain't supposed to discuss my case with people.

Yes, you right Cherry.

I said to myself; if you think you're making me mad, you're not. I'm glad he has your case because I'm damn sure tired of taking it. On top of that, if I wanted to know anything; all I have to do is look in the file case and read whatever I want. Dean and I work in the same office, 'dumb ass.'

Donna said, our driver was sitting outside. I ask Katie if she was ready to go and that we needed to put the baby down for her nap. I had some papers I needed to look over for court the next day. Katie grabbed all the baby things and said it's nice to see you Cherry and you too Bill. Donna helped Katie to the car and Harold ran out as if w e were about to leave him. He told his mama bye and that he would see her next time she came to town.

She just stood there looking as if she was going to grab his ass and say you're staying here with me but she knew Dad would be on her real fast. I hugged her and told the girls I would talk to them later. When we got home Dad (said) well did you all have a good dinner? Katie said it was fine. You mean she didn't go left on anybody? Oh, you know Cherry, she was being herself. I got to go look over some papers; I'll see you all tomorrow. I left and went to my room. I know Dad asked Katie what happened. Our home was finished and we were going to move in it. Mom took sick and Dad asked us to please stay there a little longer because Mom wanted to move back to Mississippi.

Dad why do you want to move? I'm getting old and I just want to be with my family. If you want this house; you and Katie can have it but we have spent all that money for a home. Katie wants her own home. Well you talk it over with her. I'm getting tired son. Are you alright Dad? Yes son just tired. I think if I move your Mom down there she will feel better. The weather is a lot warmer than here and your grandma got that big old house down there with nobody there but them, and they're getting old too.

I don't know about Katie wanting to live here she wants her own home. Well if you don't want to live here I'll just sell the place. Henry when is the last time you heard from Judge Reid? Not since we took him home. I would like to go down and see him and see what Derry looks like now days. Dad is it Judge Reid you want to see or is it Cherry? Hell no, long as I don't hear from her ass its fine with me. (I laugh) When do you want to go? Do you have court tomorrow? "No." Well we will go down in the morning. I have to make sure your Mom is feeling okay. The next morning we got up and went to Derry. I showed Dad down town and how the town was in a square. We got out and went into the court house to see Judge Reid. He was in court and we went in to see what kind of case was going on. Dad wanted to see how he was in court because he knew how much Judge Reid drinks.

When we walked in, I be damn there sit Cherry Etta and Bill. When the Judge saw us he thought we had come for her. We came in the courtroom when he was sentencing her. He (said) 150.00 dollar fine and 150.00 dollars in court costs. When she turned around and saw us, her mouth dropped open. "What you doing here? Who called you? I said no one; we came to see the Judge. We didn't know you were in court. Dad said "What the hell have you done now? It's none of your damn business Robert. I left Oklahoma City to get away from your ass, now you coming down here to spy on me you have a woman; she ain't enough for you? Dad please, we came to see the Judge leave her alone. We went in Judge Reid's chambers. He was surprised to see us. Dad said Joe I just wanted to come see you and spend the day with you. Do you have any more court case today? Can you leave for a few hours? Yes, that was my only case today. I don't know what in the world I'm going to do with that woman. I hate to send her to the pen and I hate to lock her up in jail all the time. I know about the beating she have had and I think all those beatings are getting next to her. They picked her up last night for drunk driving and she tried to hit the officer; so they put her in jail until she cooled off. I let her out because she had to be at work early this morning. I really feel sorry for her and I know what her kids daddy did to her, I think she sorry about it, she think about it a lot she need a lot of help. Dad (said) Judge she so hard headed maybe someday she will be ok. Judge asked us if we wanted lunch and told us about a nice cafe on the north side of the square that served good food.

After we had lunch, Joe and Dad wanted to go do a little golfing. We went to the country club. I sit in the club and read some work I had in the car and had a few drinks. Some of the guys that live in Derry came by and I had a talk with them. The People in Derry were very friendly. While I was sitting there; this man walked up to me and (said) hello there young man you the young lawyer out of Oklahoma City that represented Cherry Jackson. Oh yes I remember you; you're Floyd. Yes, what you doing back here on another case? No my Dad and I just came to visit with Judge Reid. We got to get us another judge. Joe is getting to o old and he drinks a lot. Sometimes he's drunk up there in court. He handles only small cases now. We just let him come in for a few hours, now. I heard Cherry moved back here. Have you seen her since you been here? Yes.

They hired her back down there at the Bus Station. She is a good cook. I go there all the time. She doesn't act the same since she moved back here but some days I go down there and she act a little crazy. Floyd what changed your mind about Cherry case? When Ethel got up there and said what she said, I felt sorry for them kids and the way he mistreated her and the kids don't need a man in their lives like that and that poor girl of hers is scared of her own daddy. I thought about Joe's son coming up dead and Joe thinks he did it. Joe really loved that boy he had by Ethel. Well good to see you son. If I ever need a good lawyer I sure am going to call you. Thank you, Floyd.

It was getting late and I wanted to get back home. Judge Reid wanted us to come in and have dinner with him or a few drinks. We had a couple of drinks and told him we had to leave. I drove by Cherry's house to tell her good bye and to let Dad see where she lived. The place looked nice. The outside had flowers and lawn chairs. I guess Bill is a nice man. The lady next door said Cherry was not home and that she always goes to the Devil Den every Saturday night on Ash Street. That is where you will find her. Where is it? Oh down there by the tracks as you leaving town, cross the track, and turn right, you can't miss it. After you cross the track, ask anybody.

I told Dad I think I knew where it was and that I remember seeing the sign. When she got out of jail; we all went and ate soul food. We pulled up, got out and everyone outside was looking at us. Someone said, You boys looking for somebody? Yes, Cherry Etta Jackson, is she in there? Nobody said anything. When we walk up to the door there she was out on the dance floor. I mean she was dancing so hard she didn't even see us walk in. Bill saw us and he got up and came over to us. Hi, how you guy's doing? Come to see Cherry. Come on let me buy you a drink. Everybody's eyes were on us. The place was full. She was dancing on a record call, "Do the hot gun baby". She was so drunk I never saw her that drunk before, she looked up and saw us and she came unglued.

"What the hell you doing in here still spying on me I though you left town. I told you I moved here because I can do what the hell I want and I don't have to have no damn body telling me how I should live. I'm the boss in my house; not that damn Donna. I'm happy here you two have done enough for me. You took my kid's and turned them on me and Robert you brought me to Oklahoma and put my ass out on 2nd street and left me for that damn, Becky. I'm the one you should have, put me in that damn big house I should have been there instead of Becky Sue. I should have been rich. You should have given me that money and I wouldn't have to work. You turned your damn back on me. I ain't got shit. So take your ass back to Becky Sue and leave me the hell alone. Dad (said) her name is Becky Ann. Whatever Sue or Ann you need to go home to her and stop spying on me. I'm doing well without you. I got me a good man now who loves me.

Bill said, Cherry come on let me take you home, you've had enough. I ain't going nowhere till I get ready. No man is going tell me what to do no more. Dad said I should have left your black ass in Mississippi. Yes! You should have because I ain't been nothing but hurt ever since I been here. When I was in Mississippi I was treated well. All I had to do was say yes ma'am, no ma'am, yes sir, no sir. The owner came over and said would you gentlemen like to have a drink? No we're leaving. Yes take your ass out of here and leave me alone. Bill said I'm sorry she's drunk I know she don't mean what she saying. In the morning she will be sorry she said that. Dad (said) Bill you tell her I said keep her ass down here if I see her back in Oklahoma City I will have her ass locked up for a long time. You kiss my ass Robert. Dad I'm so sorry I should have just went back home and said nothing to her.

We walked out and before we could get in the car Bill had her over his shoulder putting her in the car. Dad said you know son, maybe she's right. I should have been better to her. Maybe all the things that has happen to her is my fault. No Dad you have been good to her family. She chooses the lifestyle she wanted so we will leave her alone. We got back to the City and Katie and Mom was waiting for us. Mom said how did everything go? Dad (said) I don't want to talk about it. Dad went up stair. Mom (said) Henry you guys must to have seemed Cherry Etta she is the only one that could put that look on his face. Son what happen? Oh Mom Cherry being Cherry she said somethings to Dad that upset him. Where Anna? She sleeps. I want to go see her I want to hole her and love her and you to Katie. Boy was she that bad? Mom you know her don't say anything to Dad right now. I'm sure he will talk tomorrow. Katie and

I went to the bed room and I pick up my daughter and kiss her and told her no one will ever take her away from me and I told Katie I would never take Anna from her I love them to much. The next morning we all got ready for Church, Dad went in his office he always go in there when he have a lot on his mind that is where I got it from because it's quite from every one. Katie what am I going to do with Cherry she is my Mama do I just sit back and let her hung herself. Honey she is a hard headed woman look like she would be tired of men in her life, if a man mistreated me like they did her I would never want one in my life. Honey there are a lot of women that take abuse from men, some fell they not love if a man don't beat them some, women are scare of them, some women are thinking of their children they need a man to help them. Some fell they have to keep their family together, and there are some that don't take anything off a man and will take care of their family with out him. But we all fall in love with that man we want to try to make him happy. I believe Cherry still love your Daddy he was her fist love in her life and she had her first child by him, a woman always have feeling for her first love but they can go own with their lives without him in it. Baby I will never mistreat you; I will never put my hands on you because I love you too much to hurt you. You and my daughter is the most important thing in my life and I love you both so much. And we love you to Henry Lee Wilson. You know Katie I have a feeling if Cherry don't get her life together one day she will disappear and we will never find her. Oh Henry don't think like that I know she need help and I know Robert deep down Robert still love her he just don't know how to deal with her, I can tell when he look at her, I see it in his eyes he still love her and your Mom can see it to. You Mom take the insults from Cherry because she know your Dad love her Becky take care of you and your sisters and brother because deep down she know it is what your Dad wants because you mean the world to him. Your Mom love your dad, we women do a lot for our men when we love them we take a lot to try to keep peace and make you happy. Even though we take so much there is a time we give up. Your Mom is getting tired of things and she is ready to let go of everything, sometimes it's not worth it. You and your Dad don't know your Mom is in the middle trying to make you and your Dad happy with your family. Oh Katie I didn't think what Mom was going through I will do better for her, I know Mom is sick and I will have to take better care of her. Henry I think we better sell our house and stay here to help your Mom. When I go in the new house Anna, cries and cries while we are there and soon as we leave she stops. I love being here with your Mom and Dad and your mom is like a mother to me and we get along good together. I really do like this house. I like the servants and the noise around here. This is your home and I know you love it here too. Thank you Katie, I love you so much.

Three months have passed and summer had gone so fast. Shelly was getting ready to leave for Atlanta; Dad had talked her into going to Moore house College. Since she had the money to start out that we gave her, she had also won a ten thousand dollar scholarship. She was a little scared because it was the first time she was on her own. Shelly called her mama to tell her she was leaving the next day for college and wanted to tell her good bye. She said Cherry said she did not feel good and couldn't come to tell her good bye but after she got settled, she would ask Bill to drive her down to see her and for her to call her if she need anything. Shelly said she told her she loved her.

I sent my driver to go pick Donna, Carrie and Shelly up in the Limo and for him to come back and get me. Mom and Dad wanted to say good bye to her. When we drove up to Moore House Collage, there was so many kids' there; Shelly said she thinks she would like it. They thought Donna was her mother. Donna or Shelly said no different. We went to Shelly's dorm room and met her roommate and they hit it off. We told her good bye and she cried and said she would miss us. She hugged Carrie and told her to make sure she did what she was told because Donna loved her. Donna was crying, and said she hated to leave her baby. She made Shelly promise to call every day. I hugged her and told her if things didn't work out and she needed me to come; for her to call me. We got in the car and drove off and left my sister in Atlanta. After I got home no one was at home. It was our servant's day off and I wondered where everyone was. I thought they had all went to dinner. When I went to my bedroom, Katie had left a note on the bed. Henry I'm at Mercy Hospital with your Dad and Mom. She was having chest pains. Love Katie. I went to the hospital and found Katie and Dad in the waiting room. They said they had only been there about thirty minutes. They were waiting for someone to come and tell them something. I called Dean from the hospital and told him about Mom. "Henry, I'm on my way." Dad wanted to know how was my trip and if Shelly like the college. I told him she was fine. I wanted to know about Mom and what had happened. "We were in the den and she said she wasn't feeling good and that her stomach was hurting. We told her it maybe something she ate and she said she was going to bed. When she got up, she said sharp pains were in her chest and it felt like something was twisting in her chest. So we brought her here. The doctor came out and said "she was having a mild heart attack" and wanted to keep her in the hospital for a few days. She will be fine; we just want to make sure, she just needs to rest. "Your wife seems a little stressed. Do you know what she stressing about?" I look at Dad and he said he didn't know.

We stayed at the hospital until late that night. Mom was doing okay. The doctor told us to go home and let her rest for the night and he would call if anything happened that we should know about. Dean came in and wanted to know what was wrong? I told him and he was sorry and wanted to know what could he do? Just being here is good. "Henry do you want me to take some of your cases this morning?" If so, I'll let you know. Once I am sure Mom is okay tomorrow, than I will know.

The next morning Dad said he had a business meeting he had to go to for a few hours before he went to the hospital. Katie said she had somethings she needed to do and she was taking Anna to her mom's house. I had to be in court all morning. I told Dad I would stop by and ask Donna if she could stay with Mom until one of us got there first. When I got to the house on 8th street, Cherry Etta' car was sitting there. When I knocked on the door, Donna came to answer it. Carrie was getting ready to leave for school. Carrie hugged me and said "Henry why you here so early? Is Shelly okay?" Cherry Etta came out of the bathroom. Henry what you doing here so early? You heard from Shelly? How is Harold is my baby okay?"

Hi Cherry, what are you doing here so early? "I came back to see how Shelly was doing I didn't get to make it before you took her off way down there away from home and left her by herself. Shelly don't know how to take care of herself, you know how hard it is for a woman by herself. Let alone on a little girl that never been away from home." I'm sure Donna taught her well. Donna I came by to ask you if you could go to the hospital and sit with Mom until Dad come. He had a meeting he had to go to and as soon as he gets out, he will be there. "Sure Henry, I would love to. I'll drop Carrie off to school. Let me get my purse. I'll come by as soon as I get out of court. If you need me, call my secretary. She will know how to reach me. Good to see you Cherry.

"What's wrong with Becky?" She had a small heart attack. "Well if her fat ass stop eating all that rich food and loose some of that damn weight; she wouldn't have had a heart attack." Don't you start any shit Cherry! "Cherry why do you always say things like that? Miss Becky is a nice woman and I love her. (Carrie said) Henry tell her I will be praying for her and I will come see her after I come home from school." Oh you can go see her but you can't come see your own mama? I'm still your mama."

Donna said "Come on Carrie, I'll drop you off at school. Cherry I need to lock my door. Lock your door you, going to locking me up in here. No! You are leaving to. Well where in the hell you think I'm going? I don't know. You don't live here anymore. You mean I drove all the way down here and I can't stay here till Carrie come home. Like I said Cherry, I need to lock my door. Henry Lee, you gone let her talk to me like that. I walk out. Henry Lee do you hear me? I kept on walking and got in my car and drove off. I didn't want to get in to anything with her and Donna. The way Cherry had been treating me and as much as I have done for her, I was tired. She can go see Dean or call him.

I thought about my Mom and I decided to go by the hospital and check on her. When I got there, Dad was there. Dad I thought you had a meeting? I do. I left home a little early to check on your Mom. Hi Mom is you feeling okay? Yes baby. I feel a lot better. I wasn't looking for you this early. I had to come by and let you know how much I love you and let you know I'm glad you're my Mother. I want you to get well and come home I miss you already. I don't know what I would do if anything happened to you. Oh baby nothing going to happen I'll be fine!

Hi Donna what you doing here? Hi Becky! I came to sit with you for a while I know you tired of Robert's bossing. (Mom laughs) you know him. Mom said you two can go on and do what you need to. Donna is here if I need anything, she w I l l call you. I kissed Mom and told her I would be back as soon as I could. Dad kissed her and told her he loves her and when she get out he was taking her on a long trip for a rest. We left. I didn't tell Dad that Cherry was in town. I went by the office to pick up some papers. When I got there, Cherry's car was there. I drove around the back and came through the back door. I didn't want to see her right now. Not after all the things she had said and I didn't feel like arguing with her.

My office is next to Dean's and all I have to do is

open one of my doors to his room. My door was open a little and I could hear him and Cherry talking. Cherry, I know Henry love you. He have a lot on his mind you should understand, Becky is the only mother he been around all his life and she raised him. He can't help from loving her, ever since Henry found out about you; he have been nothing but nice to you but you say things to him and to the people he love that he don't like. You need to think of other people's feelings. Henry and the Wilson's can't help what happened to you. You have to take responsibility for your actions. You can't keep putting it all on everybody else."

"Mr. Wilson wanted the best for his son. He knew Henry could make it if he lived with him and Mrs. Wilson. You should be happy that she loved your son so much she think of him as her own and not mistreat him; like some other women do their step kids. "Well when I came back, he should have let me take care of my own kids; he should have told that damn Donna to move out and let me stay. She tells me this morning that she was locking the doors to her house and I had to leave. She and Henry didn't give a damn where I went. Henry didn't say a damn thing he just got in the car, drove his ass off and never looked back to see if I was alright or not.

Cherry I can't speak for Henry but if I was in his shoes I would have never came to find you. If my mother would do the things and say the things you say to him,

I would never have her around me. You have a good son that care about you. If he didn't he would never try to help you when he did. Mr. Wilson told him not to come around you but he didn't listen. Where would you be right now if Henry wasn't in your life? Where would your kids have been when your mother died? You would have been in prison for killing your husband, if it wasn't for Henry. When your mother died, you were gone for three years. When you came back you may not have ever found your kids if Henry and his family had not been there for them. You need to get down on your knees and thank God every day for the son you have. One day if you don't straight up Henry will walk out of your life forever or never help you again. You need to get along with Mrs Wilson and Donna; those, two women mean the world to him. You have a beautiful daughter-law and the most beautiful granddaughter in the world. The way you acting they don't want their child around you when you act crazy. I'm not crazy I can't help the way I am I'm just being me. I was hurt all my life. It hurt me so much when Robert married that woman and not me. If he couldn't married me we could have work something out together. We could have seen each other some kind of way he didn't have to do me the way he did. All those men I met didn't mean nothing to me I never loved them like I did Robert. Yes them other men beat me raped me mistreated me, but Robert broke my heart how can you fix a broken my body heal from what the other men did to me, but not Robert when I'm around him I say things and do things to try to get back at him. I say things to Becky because I know it make him mad. Cherry you have to leave Mrs Wilson out of this mess she had nothing to do with what Mr Wilson did to you. All men want their son is their life no matter if they good or bad. Mr Wilson was only 0 Dean I have so much bitterness and hate in my heart I don't know how to let go. Cherry do you know God? Do you go to church? For what church can't help me. No but God can if you believe in him, I bet if you start going to church it will make you feel so much better and he sure can help heal your broken heart. What good is going to do for me I see people going to church and them at the Devil Den drinking just as much as I do and then go to the church the next morning with a hangover and sleep and sing in church like they ain't done anything wrong? I don't know if going to church will help me. You know Dean I do hope Becky get better I don't want anything to happen to her Do you think I should go see her and tell her I'm sorry for being mean to her. No Cherry, Henry and Mr Wilson is there and she need all the rest she can get, you know if Robert see you there he will get to cussing and make her feel bad, so just leave things along. Well I guess I'll just go back to Derry I know it will make them all feel good if I never come back or disappear again, I ain't nothing but trouble to them I ain't crazy I see how they all look at me. I cry almost every night for what I did and how I lost my kids because of some crazy ass man that took me away from them. Now they don't love me you know how much that hurt me. All the one's I love is out of my life They all go to dinner together they all welcome in that big beautiful house and I ain't, never put my foot in there they never ask me to come in how do you think that make me feel? One of these days I might just walk is there and say hello Mrs. Becky, I bet she will die of a heart attack right then and there. No Cherry don't you ever do that. Well they all think I'm crazy I might show them all how crazy I am. Cherry you know Henry love you and he know you love him. It was a big shock to him to fine out you were his real mother. The woman he knew all these years he call Mom and finding out she wasn't he was hurt to, but he came to you to help you, and he still helping you and your kids whenever you need him for anything. He and Robert is helping sending your daughter to the best college Harold haven't been is trouble since he been with him. What more do you want from him? I want to live in that nice house that he bought for Donna it should be mines. Cherry if you didn't leave with that man you would have been in that house it's not Henry fault it's yours. Dean how come you not married are you gay or something? No Cherry I'm not gay I'm looking for the right woman like your son did.

Bye Dean I'm going home back to Derry. You be careful here is some money to help you out and on gas.

Thank you Dean, Henry really lucky to have a friend like you tell him I said good bye and when I come back it will be to take Carrie and Harold with me. Cherry you leave them along there is no way Mr Wilson will let you have Harold he love him and Harold love him, Carrie is happy with Donna just leave them along and go back to Derry and try to be happy. Well, been nice talking to you Dean I'll think about what I going to do about my life from now on. I didn't let Dean or Cherry know that I was listening to what they were talking about I went back out the back door and I saw Cherry driving away. I started to cry I guess I do love Cherry. I thought about Mom and I went to the hospital to see about her, when I got there Dad and Barbara was there. Barbara ran and hugs me. Hi Henry you not going to work today. No I wanted to check on Mom. I gave Mom a big hug and keep hugging her. Baby you alright. Yes Mom I love you so much and I want you to get out of this hospital as soon as you can. It's nice we all here together I guess I had to get sick for all of us to be together at the same time. Oh Mom you just get well. I will baby. The doctor came in and said Mom was doing better and she could go home as soon as she could get dress if she promises she would lose some weight and take a long walk every day. He was putting her on a different medicine. Thank you Doctor. Dad and I step out so Barbara could help Mom get dress. We took Mom home and I help put her in bed, she was so glad to be home. Barbara told her that she was going to stay a few more days with her. When I went in the Office the next day Dean told me Cherry came by before she left and told him she was still in love with Dad. I didn't tell him I overheard them talking. I told Dean how much I love his friendship and for taking time to listen to Cherry Etta. I feel sorry for her but there is nothing I can do to get her and Dad back together. It's been two weeks and Dean said he hasn't heard from Cherry Etta. When I got home Katie said Judge Reid call and wanted me to call him. Is he alright? I call Judge Reid and (said) Judge you alright how is everything. Son it's about your Mama, she is back in jail she was arrested last night, her and her boyfriend got in to it and he left her at the Devil Den across the track. She was drunk and waking home she got to the stop sign and a girl in a car drove up and said what you doing out this late nigger. Cherry said it made her so mad she grab the girl hair with her left hand and was holding on to the girl hair and beating her with her right hand, the car was still running and Cherry was drag and still holding on to the girl hair and they hit a park car. Cherry got a few starches and bruises on her. I think she will be okay. I will make sure she's alright. The girl came to the police station and fill charges on her. Police said your Mama was real drunk. I just call to let you know I have to charge her for assault and battery, I'm going to keep her in jail for a while to let her know she have to stop getting drunk so much I'm not going to charge her a fine and I'm letting you know not to come get her out I'm not letting her out right now. Thank, you Judge for calling me. Henry she will be treated alright in jail I'll see to it, tell your Dad he have to come back and play golf with me. I will Judge, good bye. I told Katie why Judge Reid called. Henry is there something you can do for her. No I'm not and I'm telling Dean not to this time Cherry needs to grow up. Katie you know what I want to do right now. I want you and Anna to get ready and we are going flying to Florida I want to just lay on the beach and drink and spend some quite time with you. No Cherry no Dad, no Dean, no one but you come on let's leave I'll call and have the jet ready and we can buy new clothes and everything we need get Anna. The phone started to ring and ring hello oh hi Dean what's up. Henry I just got a call from Cherry and she want, me to come get her out of jail. I told Dean what Judge Reid said and that I was going to Florida and would, he take care of my cases. Dean said he wanted to go too. No Dean Katie is going with me we need some time together. Katie, Anna and I just left and went to Florida We were only gone for four days it was so nice to rest and not be bother with anyone. Soon as I got back my secretary said Cherry been call me to come get her. She was real mad because she couldn't reach me. I didn't want to be bother with Cherry tell her I'm out of town. When we got back Dean told me he ran into one of his old girl friend from high school and they had a few dates while I was gone.

Dean ask me if Katie and I would go to dinner with him and his friend he wanted us to meet her. The next day we went to dinner. Dean introduced us and her name is Rachel. We had a nice dinner we dance and talk for hours I like Rachel and so did Katie. Dean was so happy. It's was late when we got home we went to bed. The next morning when we got to the breakfast table Mom and Dad was there. Mom (said did you two have a nice time)? Yes Mom Dean bought his new girlfriend she seem nice. Dad (said) Your Mama been calling for you she said Dean won't answer his phone and she want to know what in the hell wrong with you two and for you to answer your damn phone and she slam the phone down. I guess she may be in trouble, that's the only time she calls. I told her you guys were out of town and won't be back for a few months. She said all of you kiss her ass, she was mad. I told Dad she was back in jail and Judge Reid wanted her to stay in there for a while. Cherry was still in jail after four weeks Bill call and said Cherry want me to please come get her out and she said they told her the only way she can get out she would have to have a lawyer, she said for you or Dean come get her out now. Bill, tell her I can't get her out until they set a bond for her and Dean can't get her out either. Henry I don't think she will like that. Well tell her she need to stop doing so much stupid ass shit. A month later Judge Reid told Cherry she had to tell the girl she was sorry and pays the girl doctor bill, Cherry was also put on one year spender sentence if she got in any trouble she would spend a year in jail. When she got out she came to Oklahoma City to my office and when she walked in the door she started to cussing me and calling Dean and I so many dirty names, we thought she was going crazy. (She told Dean) you know you could have bought your sugar ass to get me out of jail. I need two hundred dollars to pay that girl doctor bill I don't have money. Dean told her he wasn't giving her a damn thing nice as he been to her and she have the nerve to cuss him out and then ask him for money she can go to hell and walk out the door. She looked at me and said you know one of you could have come and got me out of that damn nasty ass jail. Henry I'm your mother how could you let me stay in there so long. I'm tired of you all putting me to the side, if you didn't want to help me you could have sent someone or gave Bill the money to get me out. That bitch had no business calling me out of my name she didn't have to say anything to me. I wasn't doing anything to her, she got what she deserves. I set there and just looked at her and thought how could she come in my office cuss Dean and me out Dean and I was also nice to her I wanted to grab her and kick her ass out of my office, but I said to her leave my damn office and don't bring your ass back. She hull of and hit me in my back as hard as she could and said don't you ever talk to me like that next time I" kick your ass do you hear me boy. She got to the door and turn around to me all of you fuckers can kiss my black ass I won't come back and I won't ask you for nothing I don't need none of you bastards. I knew then I didn't want her in my life and I wasn't helping her any more. On the way home I thought about all the beating those men gave her and I know she was going crazy. When I walk in the door Dad said what's wrong with you look like you want to kill someone is it your Mama. Oh Dad I'm just tired,(I told him) about Cherry getting out of jail and what she did and what Judge Reid did to her and she coming here and cussing Dean and I for not getting her out. Henry I want you to let me take care of Cherry from now on when she get in trouble again I'll take care of everything she is my reasonability I'm the one who bought her here from Mississippi. The next day Dad went to Derry and said he visited with Judge Reid they played golf and he had a long talk with him about Cherry Etta, he went by Cherry Etta and had a talk with her before he came back home and said Cherry won't be bothering us anymore. Dad what did you do to her did you kill her? No son. It's been four months and I haven't heard from my Mama Cherry Etta. I called Judge Reid and ask him about her, he said he haven't, seen her. Whatever my Dad said to her must have work. It's was fall break and Shelly came home we were all so glad to see her; Donna was like a proud Mama. Shelly asks Donna if she could use her car to go to Derry to see Cherry Etta because she haven't seen or heard from her since she left for college. Harold and

Carrie said they wanted to go with her because they haven't heard from her. Shelly said when they got to Cherry Etta house she was in bed. Bill told them she drink every day and lost her job at the bus station, he said she said she drink because she lost you kids and she don't think you all love her anymore. I take care of her and try to make her happy I do everything for her but she cry a lot and just drink and sleep all day I think your Mama is sick in the head she do so many stupid thing around here she need help I think she need to be put somewhere where she can get help. Shelly went in the bed room and said Mama wake, up this is Shelly, get up. (Shelly said) Her Mama said leave, me the hell along get out of here and don't bring your ass back and she turned over. Bill told Shelly he took Cherry to the doctor and they are running test on her and they will let her know when they find out. Thank you Bill will you call us and let us know what is going on, we will be back before I go back to college. Bill told Shelly that she talks, all the time about you kids and how much she loves you. Shelly Harold and Carrie came back to Oklahoma City, they said they felt sorry for their Mama and will go see her more often maybe she would get herself together. I was through with Cherry I didn't care anymore what happen to her I went on about my life and taking good care of my family. Harold and Carrie were taking good care of and Shelly was doing fine in college. Shelly was getting ready to go back to college fall break was over she wanted to go back to Derry and see her Mama. They all got in the car and went back to Derry I didn't want go because I didn't want to hear Cherry cuss me out again. Hour later Shelly call me crying so hard I couldn't understand what she was saying. Shelly calm down what's wrong? What in the hell Cherry do to you? Henry, Mama going to kill me, we at the hospital in Derry. Shelly I'm on my way I'll be there as soon as I can. Katie and Dad said what the hell going on? I told them I didn't know Shelly was crying so hard she couldn't talk. (Dad said) That damn Mama of hers, I'm putting her in the nut house she better not hurt those kids. When we got to the hospital in Derry, Shelly came running to me and put her arms around me Henry I'm so sorry I didn't mean to do it. Do what? Dad said Shelly where is your Mama, Shelly kept crying Dad put her in his arms and I run to the desk and ask what in the world happen. The lady at the desk said sir who are you. I'm their damn brother. And don't you tell me you can only talk to her family I am their family. They were in a car accident and Harold was hurt real bad. How bad? Sir Harold was killed. I started to scream and fell to my knees Dad and Katie ran over to me. Son what happen please tell me where is Harold and Carrie? He is dead he was killed in an accident. It's was the first time in my life I saw my Dad break down and cry he said no God no, God not my Harold I know you didn't take my son. Where is Carrie? They said she was still in the emergency room. We ask

Shelly if she could calm down and tell us what happen. The police came over and said you friends of the family? Yes, yes what happen? Some witness at the scene said a big truck was changing lane and hit the car, the car turn over and Harold was thrown out of the car he died at the scene. The doctor came and wanted to know if we were Carrie family, he said Carrie would be okay she have a lot of bruises and in a lot of pain but she will be okay she have a big knot on her head we going to keep her overnight. Dad (said) have anyone let Chery Etta know. No Dad I'll go tell her and bring her to the hospital. Son you stay and I'll go get her she won't act a fool with me I'll take care of her. No Dad I want to. When I got to My Mama house before I got out I said God please let me say the right words to her, God how do you tell a mother her child is dead? What in the world is she going to say to me? When I got to the door I stood there for a few minutes before I knock. When I knock Bill came to the door Hi Henry how you get here so fast I know about the accident Cherry is sleep and I didn't know what to say I was waiting for her to wake up she will be in a better mode when she wake up on her on. I'll tell her, I went in Mama, room she was snoring so hard. I touch her and said Cherry, Cherry wake up this is Henry Lee wake up I have something to tell you. She opens her eyes and said Henry what you doing here? What time is it? It's two o clocks. Is everything alright what you doing here this time of day? Mama get up I need to talk to you. She looked at Bill and said what the hell you call my son and tell him on me? Bill didn't say anything. Mama the kids was coming to see you before Shelly go back to college. Bill told me they came and I didn't wake up, so they come back to see me are they out in the car tell them come on in. They not here they are in the hospital. Cherry jump up in the hospital what they doing in the hospital? They were in a car accident. Are they okay you came to get me to take me to the City? No Cherry they are here in Derry Shelly came back to see you and Harold and Carrie wanted to come with her they were in a car accident outside of Derry and Harold was killed. Cherry just looked me in my eyes and said nothing she keep looking at me and then tears started running down her face, she wouldn't take her eyes off me.

Shelly felt so hurt I just put my arms around her and she still said nothing. Cherry Shelly and Carrie is at the hospital I came to get you to take you to them. do you want to go. Yes I'll go. Cherry and Bill got in the car with me and we left for the hospital. When we got there I help my Mama out of the car. When we walked in Shelly ran to Cherry and she was still crying Cherry hug Shelly and Shelly told her what happen. I'm sorry Mama I'm so sorry. Cherry put her arms around Shelly and said baby it's not your fault don't blame yourself. Where is Carrie, how is she? They said they will come and let us know when they put her in her room. Dad went over to Cherry and put his around her and said Cherry I'm so sorry can

I do anything for you. No Robert you done enough. Dad eyes was so full of tears he loved Harold. He told Cherry he would take care of everything. We all looked at her and wonder if this really Cherry Etta Jackson not blaming anyone (she said) it's all my fault if I had been a better mother to you kid, this would have never happen God is punishing me for what I've done wrong in my life. If I had never moved back to Oklahoma City, and kept you kids with me here in Derry, this would have never happen it's all my fault Harold is dead Oh God my baby, my baby is gone because of me. I need to see Harold where is he? We will find out Cherry. Thank, you Robert. They said Carrie was in her room and we can go see her. Cherry (said) baby how do you fell, can I get you something. Mama where is Harold is he alright? Don't worry baby you try to get you some sleep I'm here for you we will talk later. Carrie face was swollen she had a lot of cuts on her face and her arm was swollen real big she said she was in pain. Dad came back and said we couldn't see Harold he was mess up to bad, and they were waiting for the corner. His body would be taken to Brown Funeral Home. The nurse came in and said Miss Jackson I'm sorry about your loss, Carrie need to rest. My name is Henry Lee, I'll be at Judge Reid house, you can call me there or you can call her mother. Shelly, do you want to go back to the City or stay here with us. No I'm not leaving Carrie; I'm not leaving Harold I need to be here. Henry I'll stay with Mama until Carrie comes home and

I need to See Harold. I took Cherry and Shelly home. I would be back the next morning to get her. Dad said he was going back to the city he wanted to be with Mom when He tells her and Donna. Katie said she would ride back with Dad to check on Anna. Katie wanted to know if I wanted her to stay with me.

No baby you ride back with Dad and help him with Mom and Donna. I went to Judge Reid house and told him about the accident and ask if I could spend the night with him. Dad called me at Judge Reid house after he got home (he said) he told Mom and Donna Harold died in the accident and Mom bust in tears and cried out oh my God not my Harold She wanted to know about Cherry Etta and to see if there was anything she could do for her. She wanted him to bring her to Derry to be with me. (Dad said) I told her Cherry was sad but I was surprise how she taking it. (Mom said) Cherry was in shock and it will not hit her until the next day. I stayed in Derry with Cherry to help her. The next day I drop Shelly at the hospital to be with Carrie. Cherry and I went to the funeral home. Cherry stood up and just cried so hard; I put my arms around her. We made Harold arrangements and four days later we had his funeral at Mt Olive Church. Mom didn't come to the funeral because she fainted after Dad told her about Harold. Mom health wasn't good. Dad, Donna and Katie came. Shelly ran to Donna and (said) Donna I'm so sorry about your car I don't know where it is. Donna told her, baby

I don't care about that car I just thank God you girls are safe. I'm so sorry about Harold she and Shelly hug each. Donna (said) Cherry is there anything I can do for you I'm so sorry about Harold. Cherry looked at Donna as if she wanted to kill her Cherry (said) if you didn't let Shelly drive that damn car none of this would have happen. Donna (said) Cherry this is not the time I'm here for you and the kids, let's put our different a side for now If I had known this would happen, no I wouldn't let them come to see you. When it was time to view the body Cherry lost it she scream and scream and cried out Mama, Daddy please take care of my baby he on his way up there with you. Mama I'm on my way to be with you. I got up and put my arms around her and told her it would be alright she still had me and the girls. I would always be there for her till the end. The usher took her out and she was fighting all the way. After the funeral Judge Reid wanted all of us to come to his house for dinner. He told Cherry he would love to have everyone at his house. Cherry did not say much we though she was still in shock, she didn't eat much she kept looking at all of us as if she wanted to kill us. Shelly and Carrie told their Mama they were so sorry but they were going back to Oklahoma City and they would be back to see her later. Cherry eyes were so full of water and she looks so sad. I went over to her and told her she could come with us and stay with me and Katie as long as she wanted. Dad said to me boy are you crazy hell no. Cherry said no I don't want to ever see you crazy bastard for the rest of my life stay away from me if anyone of you come near me I will blow your damn heads off one by one. Cherry turned around and started running down the street. Cherry, Cherry come back please, my Dad hug me and said let her go. We all got in the car and came back to Oklahoma City. I was so tired I told Katie I wanted to go back to Florida for a few days Mom and Dad went to Mississippi Mom looked so tired I knew how much she loved Harold I was hoping the trip would help her feel better. Dean took care of my cases. Shelly went back to college. Carrie was doing fine but she was unable to go back to school because of the swelling. Donna said she would go to the school every day to get her homework. When we came back from Florida Mom and Dad came back the next day. He said he had to take Mom to the doctor and they found a tumor in her breast and one near her bladder. We were so upset we just lost Harold. Mom had her breast removed and the tumor. Barbara came back home to help take care of Mom and Donna help a lot. A few days later I call Cherry to see if she was okay and there were no answer. Weeks went by and no one heard from her, I started to get worry I call Judge Reid to send someone out to check on her he told me she had moved and no one knew where she was. When she needs money or anything she would call Dean, Dean said he hasn't heard from her. I stop trying to find her because it wasn't the first time she disappeared. We went on with our lives but I still wonder what ever happen to my mama Cherry Etta' I was working hard taking all the cases I could get to try to stop thinking of my Mamma, but it was hard every day I was wondering if she was dead or alive because she haven't call for money or help. God where is she is she okay? It's been a year and we still haven't heard from Mama. Mom took sick again and she wasn't getting better she told Dad she want to move to Mississippi because she didn't think she will live long and she wanted to live where she could be close to Barbara. Dad said he was tired of Oklahoma and wants to move back to Mississippi. 3 month later they went back to Mississippi. Two month later Mom died. Donna, Cherrie and Dean flew down together for the funeral, the next day Shelly came. It's was so sad but we were happy we were all together the house was so full of love that we were there. Dad was so happy to see the girls. Katie, Donna, Shelly and Carrie went looking over the house and finding out what room they wanted to stay in. Dad, Dean and I just fix us drinks and talk. Mom didn't want a big funeral. Half a block from the house is our family cemetery. We all walk to the cemetery a few of the servants were there and the minister. Donna sang a beautiful song and we all said something about Mom. Dad wanted all of us to stay a few days with him. We all stayed three days I had to get back to Oklahoma City for a real big court case; Dean had to get back also. It was Sunday the servants were off and Dad wanted to take all of us to lunch before we leave. Dad got a room at the restaurant so we all could be together. After we were all served and sitting around talking. Anna said she was going to the restroom. Just a few minutes later she came back saying "she here," she here I saw her. I said calm down she who? Grandma Cherry she is in the rest room she gave me a hug and said she was happy to see me and what was I doing here, I told her Grandma Becky died and she said she was sorry to hear it and she ran out. Where did she go? I jump up and went to the rest room but she was not in there. I went back and ask Anna was she sure. Yes daddy it was her. We didn't see Cherry anywhere. When we were leaving Anna said Daddy that is the lady I saw. It was a picture of Cherry on the wall saying employee of the month. I went to the desk and ask the lady where were the lady on that picture. *(She said) Oh you talking about Cherry she just left for the day. Can you tell me where she lives?* No I'm sorry I can't she off for the next two days you can come back to see her is anything wrong sir. No I just wanted to talk to her. I'll tell her you want her can I have your name? No I'll come back. Dad couldn't believe she had moved back to Mississippi that is why we couldn't find her. When we got back to the house Dad ask the servants if they knew where she lived. No one knew where she lived. Everyone said they wanted to stay two more days to make sure it was her. I stayed also after the two days we went back to the restaurant, and she wasn't there they said she call in

sick. We all had to go back home Dad said he would
keep an eye out to see if he could find her and will keep
us in touch. Dad said knowing her she may have left
town. It's been a week and Dad said no one have seen
her he think she pack up and left town that is what she
always do so he stop looking for her. I did worry about
my Mama she haven't called or try to get in touch with
any of us, I know she took it hard when Harold died, my
Dad was so sad also he loved Harold. He also been so
sad about loosening Mom they said he go visiting her
grave every day. It's been five months since I been back
to Mississippi I talk to Dad and Barbara every day. Dad
wanted all of us to come to Mississippi for Christmas.
December 25, 1954 Dad wanted the family to come to
Mississippi so we all could be together; he missed all of
us. It was so good to have all of us home at once. Barbara
surprise us with her wedding she got married the next
day after Christmas it was at the house she didn't want
a big wedding because Mom wouldn't be there. She
married a lawyer from Mississippi.

The next day the girls wanted to go shopping for
Christmas sales, when they came home and getting
out of the car there was Cherry Etta.(Dad said) What
the hell, where did they find her ass. Cherry Etta kept
standing by the car Katie caught her by the hand and
was bringing her to me Henry look who we found. I was
glad to know she was still alive I didn't know if to hug
her or walk away because she was a live and never try

to contact us.(Dad said) I be damn your ass still among the living, where in the hell you been and why did you run away from us at the restaurant that day? I waited for her to say something. Henry Lee Shelly and Carrie Marie I'm so sorry. When I saw Anna in the restroom, I couldn't face you all. I came back to Mississippi to try to get my life back together, I been going to a doctor here that been helping me. I don't drink any more I found me a job and I'm taking care of myself I wanted to come back and let you guys see that I had change and you girls could forgive me and let me be the mother to you when we lived in Derry. I haven't had a man in my life now since I been living here, I'm happy here my life is going so well. (Dad said)Well I be damn, Cherry you look like the girl I fell in love with years ago. We all went in the house and Cherry (said) I want to thank you so much Donna for taking care of my kids and I'm sorry for all the things I said to you will you forgive me. Donna looked shock and couldn't say a word. Henry Lee will you forgive me I love you so much son; I haven't forgot what all you did for me.

We all told Cherry: we love her and so happy she was getting her life together. Dad asks Cherry where she was staying. (She said) I'm staying with my cousin she live a mile and a half from here she some time bring me to town and most of the time I walk I'm use to walking. (Dad said) Henry can drive you home or I'll do it. No Robert I like walking. Cherry got up to leave and told the girl she hope she could see them before they left. Just before she got to the door (Dad said) Cherry why don't you stay and have dinner with us, you can spend time with your kids Carrie said please Mama, stay and talk to us you really seem like you have change. After dinner we all sit around talking. Cherry wanted to know how the girls were doing she said Carrie do you have a boyfriend I know you will be out of school this year what are your plans? Carrie said she wanted to join the Air Force. Shelly said after college she wants to go back and become a lawyer. Cherry spent the night and the next morning after breakfast she said she had to go. Dad and I walk her outside and Dad said Cherry you gone be alright. Yes Robert I'm fine. Robert after I went home after leaving Judge Reid house I was so upset that I lost Harold again, I knew I would never see him again; I was so upset I wanted to kill all of you. Three days later I got so upset all I could think of was to get even with you I came to Oklahoma City to kill you for taking my two boys they were my babies. I got some gasoline came to your house and poured it around your house, I look through your window I saw you and Becky sitting in the living room just when I got ready to strike the match I saw Harold walk in and you got up and hug him and wouldn't let him go. I knew he love you so much he came back to save your life, so I ran off and all I could do, was cry and cry I went back to Derry and pack all I could and I came back to Mississippi because I didn't won't to try to kill you again. I'm sorry Robert I was so mix up. Will you forgive me? Cherry I still love you, I came looking for you one day Cora told me you were down on second street I knew what all went on down there and I knew you shouldn't' be there you should have been home with my son. I found you in a club call Deep Duce you had your back turn to me and you were sitting on a man lap kissing him, boy that hurt me so bad I got so mad I wanted to come over and just whip your ass but the owner a man name Donnie Hudspeth caught me by my arm and said sir I don't want trouble in here. Can I help you? I didn't know what the black folk, would do to me so I left. When I got home all I could think of was to hurt you, the only way I knew how was to marry Becky and take my son from you and not let you see him. When I was mean to you it was because I loved you so much and all I could think of was seeing you with another man, We both old now and you been through so much I just can't understand why you do so many stupid thing and say so many hurtful thing to everyone in your life and why you always pick men that always hurt you. I'm sorry Robert you saw me kissing on Tommy. I was so young and I was having fun I always wonder why you didn't want me anymore. I loved you so much all I could think of was to hurt you for taking my son from me but the only one I hurt was myself: I didn't care about myself any more I was just mad all the time and when I met my kids Dad he would beat me because of you I would tell him how much I loved you and I had my first child by a white man and he hated me for that. As the years pass my life changed I didn't care. I wanted to see Henry Lee I wanted to be in his life and that hurt me more then you will ever know. I was so jealous of Becky with my two boys loving them and let them think she was their Mama that is why I wanted to hurt her she knew they were my boys and act like they were her and Donna was the same way they made me feel like I was nothing so I act like I did to hurt all of you because none of you act like you loved me you only tolerated me. I'm so sorry Cherry, starting today Cherry I will make it up to you, you didn't deserve all the things that happen to you I'm so sorry. You know Robert all those men I was with just messed up my head. Since I came back to Mississippi and going to the doctor, it sure have help me a lot I' doing fine now. Dad walks over to my Mama and gave her a big hug and said thing will change between us from now on. I was so happy to see then together without hating each other. I saw a smile on my Dad and Mama face I never seen before. Mama,(said) Henry Lee I want you to always remember how much I love you, I want you to always keep your sisters in your life. I promise I will because they mean the world to me, and Mama I love you. For the first time I saw the biggest smile on my mama face and the hug she gave me was real love. She kept holding on to me and didn't want to let go of me. I knew then that things would be alright with us,

Cherry life had really change I'll come back tomorrow Robert and see my kids off. Sure you can. Henry drive your Mama home.(Mama said) No I'm so happy right now I just want to walk home I'll be back tomorrow. Mama started singing as she walk down the road. Dad and I watch Mama walking down the road until she disappeared. The next day we all started getting ready to catch the Air Plane back to Oklahoma City; Shelly was going back to Atlanta. We waited and waited for Cherry to come and no Cherry, Dad was getting mad because he thought she was back to her old tricks. We were getting in the car to go to the airport, Dad said Henry something is wrong I just got this feeling your Mama need help. Cherry would have come back to see you guys off, I just can't get this feeling off me. Well Dad you call me if you hear from her.

I looked at Dad and I could see his eyes felling up with water and he looked so sad. I told Katie and the girls to go on home and I will catch a later flight, I wanted to stay with Dad. Dad and I got in the car and went to find where Cherry cousin live. We found her cousin house, we both got out and knock on the door and her cousin came to the door. (Dad said) is Cherry Etta here?

No I haven't seen Cherry since yesterday she said she was going into town and she haven't come back, What do you want with her. This is her son Henry and we looking for her. Oh it's nice to meet you Henry,

Cherry told me a lot about you, when she comes home I'll tell her you looking for her. Do you have any idea where she could be? No I don't. (Dad told) her if you hear anything get in touch with him. We went back to the house hoping she made it there but no Cherry Etta. (Dad said) Son I have a bad felling about her and I never felt like this before I don't believe she ran away this time. Let's go back to her cousin house drive slow and look on the side of the road, we didn't see anything. We went back to the house Barbara said Cherry didn't come back to the house. Dad (said) if we don't hear from her by morning I'm calling the police. We went to bed around 12:00 am; Dad woke me up and said he couldn't sleep because he heard Cherry: calling him to help her. Son we got to go looking for her she need me. I never stop loving her deep down in my heart I loved her son, we both let hate come between us all I had to do was forgive her she was so young, I need to ask her to forgive me. We put out a search the next d, so many people were looking for her we went to the next town and no one could find my mama. Henry Lee your Mama act like she had really changed and I could tell she wasn't the same old Cherry, I could tell she was happy she wouldn't just leave town, she wanted to see her kids and wanted to be in your life. What could have happen to her? God where is she what happen to her, please God help, me to find my Mama please let her be okay. Two days have pass and no one seen Cherry, her cousin said she hasn't been back and she had no idea where she would be. Dad and I went back to the police station to see if they heard anything, while we were in there talking a man overheard us talking he said he saw a black lady walking down a dirt road near the bayou the other day. Do you remember what she look like? Yes she had on a red dress and a big black flop down hat, she had stop because a big old Alligator was crossing the road I slowed down, and I just went around the gator I look back and the lady was still standing there, I past a red Ford pickup truck going her way, a black man was driving it so I don't know if he pick her up or the Alligator ate her, I didn't see neither one after I look back again. Dad (said) can you take me where you saw her I'll pay you. The man and the police went to where he saw Cherry. We all got out of the cars and went looking around; we found the red dress and the black flop down hat and her shoes by the river off the road. Dad broke down and cried He said the Alligator ate her. I was so hurt oh God how am I going to tell my sisters that our mama was dead. Dad told me to wait before I call my sisters, because he wanted to find the man in the red truck to see if he saw her going to the river. We went in the black neborhood looking for a red Ford truck we asked people if they knew anyone with the red truck. As we were leaving a man walk up and said he knew a man name Zeke Turner Jr he live out by the Bayou on the old dirt road by Sunnyvale. We went back down the dirt road we past Cherry Etta cousin house just a half mile there was the red truck. We pull up to the house and before we could get out a man came out and {said} you guys lost. We got out and Dad said you Zeke Turner Jr? Yes sir I am what can I do for you? (Dad said) The other day did you see a lady walking down by Sunnyvale road? Yes you must be talking about Cherry Etta I heard she was missing. I stop and ask her if she wanted a ride home and she said no she said she wanted to walk so I drove off. Do you know Cherry? Yes I know her she live with her cousin down the road from me. Do you know where she is? No. You were the last one to talk to her what did she say to you? I ask her: if she wanted a ride and she said no and I drove off, I didn't think anything about it. I was surprise when I heard she was missing. Did you see anyone coming down the road? No. Can you think of what happen to her? I think she had to use the bathroom and when she went off the road that Alligator ate her. Dad and I left and went back to the house. Dad felt so sad, he said son I feel so bad about how I treated Cherry deep down in my heart I loved her but I was so stubborn and mad when I saw her at that Deep Duce Club with that man I couldn't forgive her. I thought she was doing fine since she moved back to Mississippi but she back to her old ways I'm through with her this time I don't ever want to see her I'm through with her crazy ass. The next morning I got ready to leave to go back to Oklahoma City, (Dad said) Henry I couldn't sleep I keep hearing your Mama calling me I need to go back and talk to that

Zeke, I think he was lying, Dad you have to let go you saw her shoes the hat and the dress she was wearing by the river. Son if the gator ate her how come her things wasn't in the river I know damn well that gator didn't put her things on the bank where they could be found. Just go back and talk to Zeke just one more time and if he can convince me he don't know anything I let it go. Please son come, go back with me before you leave. Ok Dad: come on. Dad and I went back to talk to Zeke, when we got there Zeke was getting ready to drive off. Dad jump out of the car and said I need to talk to you get out the damn car. Zeke got out and he looked real scare. (Dad said) I want you to tell me what the hell you said to her or what did you do to her and don't you lie to me, I want the damn truth.

Zeke (said) I didn't do nothing, I saw her and I stop and she was so scare of that gator in the road she jump in the car with me, she was shaking so I ask her if she would come home with me and have a drink, and she said ok. I fix her a drink and she started talking about her kids and how much she was happy to see them and she was going back the next day and see them again, she said you even made her feel good for not being mad at her any more. I like Cherry I use to ask her out and she never would go out with me, because she was in love with you so I stop asking her. When I saw her walking down the road I stop. And ask her to come have a few drinks with me. We had a few drinks and I fix us something to eat after she ate she told me to take her home. I wasn't ready for her to leave. She started telling me about how the men in her life hurt her and she didn't love any of them she said you hurt her the most when you took her son from her and wouldn't let her see him and gave him to another woman and let this woman teach him she was his mother that was why she hated your wife because she knew she wasn't his mother and she kept him away from her too. She said she hurt every day that she couldn't see her baby and this other woman taking care of her baby. She said she didn't care about herself after that and she didn't have the money to fight you for him. She loved you the most she said you were the only man she ever love and you hurt her the most. She started crying and it made me cry she said you took her other three kids from her and they turn on her for another woman. She said when her son Harold died everything in her heart died, she moved back to Mississippi to get away from all of you. When she saw all her kids that day she was happy and just wanted to walk home. She was singing all the way until she saw that gator. She: ask me for another drink. (Dad said) I don't want to hear all that shit where is she you better not lie to me I'll kill your ass right now what the hell you do to her? I'm so sorry Mr Robert, she got up to leave and she just fell down and hit her heard on the end of my coffee table I bent down to help her and she wouldn't move(I said) Cherry get up I felt her heart and I couldn't fell her heart beat, I knew she was dead.

Mr Robert I swear I did nothing to her. Where the hell is she? I took her body out back and I buried her. I saw a lizard running by so I thought about the gator in the road so I took her things and put them by the river so people would think the gator ate her. I'm sorry I didn't think anyone would believe me if they found her dead in my house because I just got out of prison for killing a woman I didn't want to go back to prison. Dad was so mad at Zeke he wanted to hurt him. When the police came Zeke show us where he buried her. Dad told Zeke to dig her up. When he dug her body up she was warped in a sheet with only her bra and panties on. I wanted to kill him when I went to him the police pull me back. The police read Zeke his rights and took him to jail. The corner came out and took my Mama body back to town. Dad cried and cried. Henry I'm so sorry for what I did to your Mama, I wouldn't forgive her I just wanted to hurt her for being with those other men. I'm so sorry. Oh God all I had to do was forgive her and we would still be together I'm so sorry. I never stop loving your Mama I was just mad at her. Oh God please forgive me for what I did to Cherry. Son I want your Mama body, put in our family cemetery. I knew I had to call the girls and Katie. I call Katie first and told her what happen and I was staying with Dad until we decide what to do, I told her I would call the girls and let them know what happen to their Mama.

The coroner, release her body and said she died of

a heart attack, when she fell the injury on her head was not deep enough to cause any trouble. Zeke did nothing to her expect buried her body. Katie the girls and Donna came back to Mississippi and we had a grave side funeral. Dad wanted Cherry body to be on the other side of him when he dies. Mom on one side he in the middle of both women. The next day we all left for home Barbara said she would take care of Dad. Dad was never the same, Barbara said he wouldn't half eat and he stayed in his room a lot. Two months later I went back to Mississippi to Zeke trial. Dad was still mad at him for what he did to Cherry. Zeke was given four years. Six months later I went back to Mississippi to bury my Dad he couldn't forgive himself for what he did to my Mama Cherry Etta. The girls and I are very close Shelly became a teacher at Morehouse College. Carrie married a retired Sargent from the Air Force and they moved to Derry in Ethel old house and fix it up real nice. Carrie had Cherry Etta old house tore down because it was down the street from her and she said she didn't want to look at it every day Cherrie have a son 6 mon old he look just like Cherry. Donna live: with Carrie they are doing fine. Dean got married and became the Governor of Oklahoma. My sister Barbara had twin boys and still live in Mississippi. Katie and I are still together and I have a son name Robert Lee and I still have my law office in Oklahoma City. Judge Reid died three months after Dad, the last time I talk to Judge Reid he said he missed

Ethel and his son so much, they found him dead because he drank himself to death. I go down on Second Street to Deep Duce to have a drink with Donnie he tell me about Mama when she would come in his Club.

"Forgiving one another is always best if not it will always hurt your heart so bad when something happen and you can't ask that person, for forgiving, God for gave you and he want you to do the same, forgiveness is so good for the soul."

Don't forget to thank Jesus today.

Wanda Rhodes

Printed in the United States
By Bookmasters